He was warrior— he was lover

In the primitive, eerie surroundings of the grotto, Diana no longer saw a reasonably civilized twentieth-century male, but a bronzed warrior.... *The muscles of his shoulders were sleek and contoured from years of violence. She shuddered at the fierce strength in him and the utter determination that blazed in his eyes.*

"Diana, what is it, honey?" Colby whispered. He gently stroked her breast, but he was aware of Diana's altered mood.

Diana blinked quickly, taking a hold of her wayward imagination. She looked at Colby and saw the affectionate concern in his eyes. The last traces of her warrior image vanished. "You feel good," she muttered as her hand moved along his back. "Warm and strong."

"Sweetheart," he breathed, just before his mouth found hers.

Diana parted her lips, inviting him into her warmth, welcoming the force of his embrace.

This time it was right. This time they were meant to be together.

Dear Reader,

What's more sensational than a new book by Jayne Ann Krentz? *Two* new books by Jayne Ann Krentz!

For those of you who have ever wished a story could go on and on, Harlequin Temptation presents two very special books from the woman whose name spells excitement. *Dreams, Part One* will sweep you away to the eerie Chained Lady Cave and a volatile, passionate love affair that takes on legendary proportions. *Dreams, Part Two* will draw you ever deeper into the tumultuous lives of Colby Savagar and Diana Prentice as they struggle to overcome dark forces in order to create their *own* destiny.

With this, Harlequin's first true series, we invite you to enjoy something a little different . . . something we've chosen to highlight for you. Each time you see this distinctive fold-back corner on the cover of a Temptation, you'll know we've discovered yet another terrific book that breaks the rules—the Editor's Choice.

And we Temptation editors would love to receive your comments on our choice. Please take the time to write to us at the following address:

Harlequin
225 Duncan Mill Road
Don Mills, Ontario
M3B 3K9
Canada

Dreams
—PART ONE—
JAYNE ANN KRENTZ

Harlequin Books

TORONTO • NEW YORK • LONDON
AMSTERDAM • PARIS • SYDNEY • HAMBURG
STOCKHOLM • ATHENS • TOKYO • MILAN

Published December 1988

ISBN 0-373-25329-X

1

HE'D HAD ENOUGH of the mating dance. He wanted her, and he was almost certain she wanted him. They weren't kids. They were mature adults. There was no need for games. He swore to himself that if she put him off again tonight, he would walk out the door. And this time he wasn't going to go back.

Even if she did make the best stir-fried vegetables in the entire state of Oregon.

Damn.

He was kidding himself and he knew it. He'd see her again tomorrow, if she politely showed him the door tonight. He'd make another date, and another one after that, until he finally got through her bedroom door.

Something about Diana Prentice fascinated him.

No, it was more than fascination. Diana Prentice was beginning to become an obsession with him, almost as much of an obsession as his writing.

He conjured up an image of her and felt the instant response of his body. At forty he shouldn't be having this kind of problem, he told himself as he shifted his position a bit to ease the sudden tightness in his jeans.

Then again, it was vaguely reassuring to know he could still suffer like this.

But why Diana Prentice?

It wasn't as if she were some young, tall, bosomy, centerfold honey pot. Diana was thirty-four, a little on the short side and built along rather compact lines.

Firm, straight nose. Assertive chin. High cheek bones. She had a smile that held a warmth of feminine secrets and a hint of mischief.

The only really spectacular thing about her was the color of her eyes. Colby was deeply intrigued by those eyes. He'd spent a lot of time trying to determine their exact shade.

He'd finally settled on the approximate description of hazel. As a writer he should have been able to do better than that, and he knew it. But it was tough to come up with a word that covered the curious blend of turquoise, green and gold that characterized Diana's faintly tilted eyes. They made him think of some exotic, mysterious feline. Sensual but untamable. She might choose to give herself to a man, but she would never be coerced or taken by him.

Her hair was an easier matter. Tawny. Definitely tawny. Pale gold layered with rich brown. Colby had been wanting to get his hands into the thick, sweet-smelling stuff for weeks. He envisioned using such a grip to hold her gently captive while he pulled her down onto a carpet of green grass and made love to her until she no longer had the strength to push him away.

Until she no longer had the energy to keep him dangling.

Until she surrendered completely.

She had to surrender to him. Why didn't she realize it? She was his. She had always been his. She could not fight him forever.

He scowled, feeling uneasy about the odd turn of his thoughts. It wasn't like him to think of a woman with such urgency and possessiveness.

The hell with it. He was brooding again.

Colby Savagar groaned and opened his eyes to study the fading light of the setting sun. Soon the mountain valley would be in deep shadow. The boulder on which he was lying was rapidly losing the heat it had been soaking up all day.

A bird wheeled overhead, searching for one last meal before seeking its nest in a towering pine nearby. Colby listened carefully and thought he heard the creature's mate calling to it, but he couldn't be sure. It was hard to hear anything up here above the waterfall. The constant roar of the foaming white water cascading down the cliff below covered most sounds.

Colby shifted position on the huge boulder, turning on his side and propping himself on one elbow. He drew up one leg to balance himself, and then he leaned over the edge of his perch to stare down at the plunging water. It was almost time for the daily light show. He didn't want to miss it.

Below him, Chained Lady Falls tore its way out of the cliffs, emerging from some mysterious source deep in the heart of the mountain. The wild water created a heavy, glistening white wall for over three hundred feet as it fell straight down to the river.

But Colby knew from previous experience that, for a few minutes, just as the summer sun set, the pristine veil would turn blood-red. The strange effect of twilight on the falls had never failed to mesmerize him.

He waited as the first tinge of color appeared in the mist that always hung around Chained Lady Falls. The sun dipped a little further behind the mountain. Brilliant gold, orange and yellow splashed across the sky. The billowing white plumes of water caught the delicate shades and reflected them. For a moment or two, gold poured from the cliffs.

The gold turned to fire a few seconds later.

And then the fire turned to blood.

Colby sat up and hooked one arm around his knee as he stared intently at the long fall of crimson water. Time hung suspended.

Then the sun disappeared completely and the falls returned to normal, pale and glistening in the evening shadows.

Colby raised his head and gazed out over the water to the roofs of the small town that clung to the banks of the river.

Maybe it had been a mistake to come back after all. What had he expected to find here? Nothing had changed in Fulbrook Corners in the past twenty years.

The falls still turned to blood at sunset just as they always had and Colby had discovered that he still hated his hometown as much as he always had.

The only thing different this summer was the presence of Diana Prentice. At the thought, Colby got to his feet and made his way over the jumble of massive rocks that marked the top of Chained Lady Falls.

Diana would be waiting for him. She had invited him over for dinner, and he had promised to bring the wine.

Colby wondered gloomily if he was doomed to spend another evening in a state of frustrated sexual tension. Then he wondered again why he was tolerating the situation.

That question was as unanswerable as the one about why he had come back to spend the summer in Fulbrook Corners.

"RELAX, SPECTER, you're going to get your dinner. You've never missed a single meal since you moved in with me, and you know it." Diana Prentice laughed affectionately at the huge brindled dog sitting expectantly beside her chair. She reached out to scratch the creature's ears and he leaned closer so that he could rest his heavy muzzle on her thigh. "Honestly, you'd think he lived on the edge of starvation."

"Maybe he did before he met you." Colby eyed the big dog with wry disgust. There was no love lost between him and the monster, and both parties knew it. They were polite enough to each other when Diana was around but that was the extent of their relationship. "Or maybe he's got a bottomless pit for a stomach. That's the ugliest dog I've ever seen in my life, Diana. No charm. No cute personality. Doesn't do any tricks. Nothing to recommend him at all. And I happen to like dogs."

Diana smiled benignly, her eyes alight with humor. "He speaks very highly of you when you're not around."

"I'll just bet he does. He'd as soon rip out my throat as look at me." Colby grinned briefly, showing his own teeth. "He tolerates me because he's afraid to offend you. He's probably worried you'd cut off his rations if he gets in the habit of tearing apart your dinner guests."

"If he's smart enough to have figured that out, then you can hardly call him a dumb dog."

"I never said he was dumb. Just very uncute."

"No," Diana agreed thoughtfully, "He's not what you'd call cute. But, then, I've never gone for cute." *If I had,* she added silently, *I wouldn't be entertaining you here in my summer cottage, Colby Savagar.*

Colby was anything but cute. Like Specter, he was strong, street-smart and no doubt dangerous when provoked. But the truth was, she didn't know much more about Colby's past than she did about her dog's. She knew Colby had an apartment in Portland, that he was forty years old, and that he looked his age. There were a number of uncompromising lines in his face.

Colby's nearly black hair was streaked with silver at the temples. It would have made him look distinguished if he'd had the kind of pleasant, regular features of most successful businessmen, doctors or lawyers. But Colby didn't have those kind of features, and the net effect of the silver in his hair was to make him look a lot like a battle-scarred wolf.

In the few weeks she had known him, Diana had never seen Colby dressed in anything but jeans, faded denim or khaki shirts and well-worn running shoes. The uniform suited him in some undefinable way.

"Where did you get the monster?" Colby asked casually, as he helped himself to more of Diana's stir-fried vegetables.

"I found him in the pound." Diana smiled, remembering. "We took one look at each other and knew it was fate."

"Uh-huh. More likely he took one look at you and knew a soft touch when he saw it. My guess is, there was probably a damned good reason why that dog was in the pound in the first place."

"He'd been abandoned." She smoothed the dog's rough fur, and Specter leaned more heavily against her leg. His watchful brown eyes looked up at her with open adoration.

"Somehow, the fact that someone had enough sense to abandon him doesn't surprise me. What is he, anyway? I mean apart from half-dragon?"

"I'm not sure. The lady at the pound said she thought he had some Rhodesian Ridgeback in him, but she didn't know what the rest was."

"I'll bet he earned his living as a junkyard dog before you got him."

Specter grinned savagely, and then tried to hide it behind a doggy yawn.

"What did you earn your living at before you became a writer?" Diana asked suddenly. Her curiosity about Colby was growing daily. She knew she was deeply attracted to him but she didn't like the idea of being attracted to what she did not understand. Diana was accustomed to being very much in control of herself and her life.

"Anything and everything that came along. I was in the army for a while. Construction work mostly after that. Then the writing started to sell."

She knew he was impatient with her questions. This was one of the few he had bothered to answer. Diana savored the small tidbit of information. "Would you like some more rice?"

"Thanks." Colby took the bowl with alacrity. "No offense, but is stir-fried vegetables and rice the only thing you know how to make? You've served the same thing every night I've been here."

Diana grinned. "It's my one and only company dish. I've never really had time to learn how to cook for guests. Besides, vegetable dishes suit me. I like to keep my weight under control."

"I guess it's a good thing I like vegetables, too." Colby sprinkled soy sauce on a fresh heap of greenery.

"Obviously Specter's not the only one around here with a hearty appetite."

"I've got an excuse," Colby said around mouthfuls of rice. "I did some climbing this afternoon."

"You climbed to the top of Chained Lady Falls again?"

"Yeah."

"You're really fascinated with those falls, aren't you?"

"One of these days I'll take you up there at twilight. It's a hell of a sight. The water catches the sun in a certain way and turns the whole thing the color of blood."

Diana shuddered. "Is that where you got the idea for the title of the book you're working on?"

"*Blood Mist*? Yeah." His hooded, gray eyes moved assessingly over her face as he put down his fork and reached for his wineglass.

Savagar's gaze had a disconcerting effect on Diana. It was one of the reasons she had been careful to keep him at arm's length since she had first met him at the post office in town a few weeks earlier. She had sensed something obscurely dangerous in that gaze, yet she had been unable to resist when he had practically invited himself over for dinner a few days later.

One dinner had led to another, and now here she was, almost a month later, playing a reckless game of sexual hide-and-seek with a man she couldn't quite fathom. Common sense warned her to sever the relationship before she was caught, but Diana found herself unable to do that. She was too attracted, too curious, too intrigued. She felt compelled to take the risk of learning more about her summer neighbor.

"What did you do today?" Colby asked, as if sensing the direction of her thoughts and wanting to distract her.

"The usual." Diana smiled and fed Specter a bite of broccoli. The dog wolfed it down as if it were a choice piece of steak. "Had breakfast, typed up some more résumés and letters to my job-hunting contacts, picked up the mail, took a long walk with Specter and read a few more chapters of *Shock Value*."

"Sounds like you're having one hell of a summer vacation, aren't you? What made you choose this burg in the first place? How come you didn't go to the coast?"

Diana shifted restlessly. She'd privately asked herself that same question more than once. "I'm not sure what made me choose this part of the state. I wanted someplace quiet. One day when I was looking at a map, I spotted Fulbrook Corners and something just clicked. I made the decision on the spot."

"And now you're stuck feeding me and trying to get through one of my novels. Fate works in mysterious ways, I guess. It's not exactly a compliment to my writing that you're taking so long to finish that book, though." Colby's mouth curved wryly upward at one corner.

Diana looked up from popping another tidbit between Specter's huge jaws. "I can't take too much of it at a time," she said honestly. "It scares me to death."

Colby shrugged. "Probably because you've never read much horror fiction before."

"I'll admit it's not my first choice of reading material. After finishing half of *Shock Value*, though, I now know why I've had the good sense to avoid the horror genre all these years. Your stuff gives me nightmares if I read it right before going to bed, Colby."

"I guess I can take some pride in that," he replied smoothly. "Scaring people is what I get paid to do."

Diana frowned. "How can you write that kind of thing? Doesn't it bother you? Don't you frighten yourself with your own fantasies?"

"When my fantasies succeed in scaring me, I know the writing is going well."

Diana shook her head, aware of a curious sense of frustration. "I doubt if I'll ever completely understand how your mind works."

"Is that a problem?" Colby asked softly. He leaned back in his chair, stretched out his legs under the table and swallowed the last of his wine. His gaze was sharp and questioning under half-lowered lashes. "Is that why we're playing this look-but-don't-touch game? You're trying to figure out how my mind works before you'll let me take you to bed?"

Diana became very still. Under her palm Specter came to attention. The dog glared at Colby with accusing eyes as if daring him to make any further offensive moves.

"I wasn't aware we were playing a game," Diana said, mustering the sort of composure that had always served her well in the business world. "I thought we were becoming friends. If you feel I'm playing games, perhaps you'd prefer to leave."

Specter didn't growl, but his lips retracted just far enough to show his teeth.

Colby glanced down at the dog and then back at Diana. "Forget it," he said, sounding half-amused. "You're not getting rid of me that easily. But I'm not going to let you off the hook, either. You know damned well you've been doing your best to keep me dangling since the first day we met. You let me get just so far and no farther."

Diana surveyed him, rapidly growing annoyed. "I see. You're not interested in developing a friendship, then? You've been inviting yourself over for dinner several times a week because you're restless and bored? You think things might be a little more amusing here in Fulbrook Corners this summer if you had a convenient bed partner?"

Colby eyed her for a long moment. "For the record," he finally said carefully, "I have never found Fulbrook Corners amusing, with or without a bedmate."

Diana flushed, sensing the savage intensity behind the words. "Then why did you come back here after being away for nearly twenty years?"

Colby leaned forward and folded his arms on the table. "I've already explained why I'm here. I have to make a decision about what to do with Aunt Jesse's house, and I needed a quiet place to finish *Blood Mist*. I decided to kill a couple of birds with one stone this summer."

"I think there's more to it than that."

Colby shook his head slowly. "You can think whatever you like. But I'm warning you, Diana. I have no intention of letting you entertain yourself this summer by trying to see what makes me tick."

"No problem," she retorted. "I'm sure I can find better things to do with my time, anyway. I've told you I've got some major career decisions to make this summer and I will no doubt be much better off if I concentrate on them instead of on you. Let's just call it quits here and now. We both made a mistake. Our judgment was off. It happens, even at our ages." Her smile was all challenge as she got to her feet and began collecting the dishes. "Dessert?"

"Yeah, I'll take dessert." Colby's voice was a low growl as he surged to his feet directly in Diana's path. He reached for her, pulling her roughly into his arms.

"*Colby.*" She spread her fingers across his chest as she fell against him. Her eyes flashed with anger.

Specter gave a fierce, disapproving whine as Diana struggled to find her balance.

"Call off your dog," Colby ordered, his mouth hovering an inch above Diana's.

"Why should I? He's only trying to protect me."

"You don't need protection from me. You can take care of yourself. Tell him to get lost."

Diana hesitated momentarily, dazed by the implied threats, both human and canine, that seemed to cloud the air around her. Then common sense took hold.

"Easy, Specter," she said firmly. "That's a good boy. Go lie down, Specter. Everything is fine. Go on, boy. Lie down."

The big dog looked unconvinced. He studied his mistress as she stood locked in Colby's embrace. Then the animal swung a deeply suspicious gaze on Colby.

"Go on," Colby said. "You heard the lady. Go lie down. I'm not going to hurt her."

With one last, complaining growl, Specter turned reluctantly and slunk off toward the corner of the room.

There he obediently settled down, but he didn't take his eyes off Diana.

"You're making him nervous," Diana said. "You're also making me nervous."

"We're even. You've been driving me crazy for the past few weeks." Colby slid his fingers into her hair, tugging the tawny mass free of its knot. "I've been wanting to do that for a long time," he added in satisfaction as Diana's hair tumbled down over his hands. He bent his head as he used his thumbs to tip up her chin.

Diana was suddenly breathless. The dark, mysterious fate she had been tempting for a month had finally cornered her. After putting off the inevitable for so long, she was awash with a reckless desire to surrender to it, to experience it completely.

Colby groaned as Diana lifted her arms to encircle his neck. "That's it, honey. Now you're catching on. That's the way it's supposed to be. Why the hell have you been so damned stubborn and elusive this past month?" His mouth came down on hers with swift eagerness, and he crushed her against the lean, taut length of him.

The kiss was exactly what she'd been expecting and yet stunningly unexpected. The intimate caress was exotic, almost alien, yet the most natural thing in the world.

It was as if Colby were some strange new masculine life form she had just encountered. Yet it was as if she'd known him well in some other time and place—had known him and feared him. *And fought him.*

He tasted the way Diana had known he would taste, and at the same time his mouth was new and strange and beguiling. He was as demanding as she'd guessed he would be, but she discovered within herself a rash need to meet his demands with a few of her own.

Colby's arms tightened around her and Diana felt the hardness of his lower body thrusting against her softness. He wanted her and he was making no secret of it. Something snapped within her, and the fiery kiss threatened to roar out of control. It was as if she had been waiting for this man and this kiss all her life.

Diana was only dimly aware of the sliding, gliding, exploring movement of Colby's hands as he moved his palms down her body to her hips. She felt his fingertips brush the curve of her breasts en route, and a sensual warmth filled her. When he cupped her buttocks and brought her more tightly against his hardened body, Diana shivered and cried out softly.

He freed her mouth with slow, drugging reluctance and began talking to her as he tugged her shirt out of her trousers.

"I knew it would be like this with you," Colby muttered as he inhaled the fragrance of her hair. His hands were trembling with the force of his desire. "Hot and sweet and frantic at first. I feel like I've been waiting for you for a long, long time."

"Oh, Colby, I wish . . ."

"Shush. Don't try to talk. Not now." He drew a thumb across her parted lips and his eyes burned as he looked down into her questioning face. "This first time is going to be fast and hard and wild. But later we'll take it slow and easy, I promise. Hell, later we'll become connoisseurs. But not this first time. I'm too hungry for you this time." His hands were moving up beneath her shirt now, seeking the gentle curves of her breasts.

The tiny snapping sound of her bra fastener as it came unhooked was what pulled Diana back from the brink. She blinked rapidly, trying to unfog her mind. She was aware of a curiously scattered sensation as if important parts of her were spinning wildly, uncontrollably. She wondered fleetingly if this was how the moth felt when it approached the flame.

Primitive, feminine instincts took over, jerking her back to safety.

"No." Her voice was a soft, beseeching thread of sound. "No, Colby," she said again, this time more firmly. "Not now. Not tonight. I don't...I'm not ready. I want to think. This isn't what I . . ."

He silenced her with an impatient kiss and his palms covered her taut nipples with deliberate possessiveness. "I want you."

"That's not enough."

"You want me."

"That's still not enough. Please let me go, Colby."

For an instant Diana wasn't sure he would release her. She knew with unnerving certainty that if he did not, she would be drawn back to the edge of the abyss, and this time she would go over into the velvet darkness with him.

She wasn't ready for that. Not yet. There was too much she did not know or understand about him.

And then, without any warning, she was free. Colby swung around and strode violently away from her, one hand raking through his dark hair. He halted in front of the cottage window and stood staring out into the night.

Specter watched him closely but didn't move.

"What is it with you, lady?" Colby said without turning around. The rigid line of his broad shoulders gave undeniable evidence of his volatile mood. "Why the constant come-on and then no follow-through? That's an adolescent's game. You're no kid."

Diana closed her eyes. "No, you're right about that. I'm not exactly a kid." She opened her eyes, and gazed at his back. "But, then, neither are you. Why the heavy pass followed by the macho temper tantrum when I fail to put out, as the kids say? You're forty years old, Colby. Too old to be acting like a teenager who isn't getting what he wants in the back seat of a car."

Colby whipped around, gray eyes lit with an unreadable combination of emotions. "Sorry," he said laconically. "Guess I misread the signals."

"I guess you did," she snapped, her heart sinking. This wasn't the way she wanted the evening to end.

He didn't move. For a long moment they simply stared at each other, neither offering a graceful way out of the highly charged situation.

"What do you want from me?" Diana finally asked helplessly. "A couple of quickies? A one-night stand?"

"Do I look stupid? Nobody with a brain larger than a cockroach's does one-night stands these days."

"True," Diana agreed readily. "So what do you want?"

"Isn't it obvious?" He shoved his hands into the back pockets of his jeans, and began to pace restlessly back and forth across the small room. "I want an affair with you."

"A few days? Weeks? Maybe the whole summer?"

He shot her a glowering look. "Yeah, maybe the whole summer. Maybe longer. As long as it lasts, for pete's sake. As long as it's good for both of us. Damn it, who the hell can answer that kind of question? Do you always have to have answers?"

Diana laced her fingers together and glanced down at them. "I'm a businesswoman," she explained with soft apology. "I like answers. I tend to look before I leap."

"Do you grill every man who takes an interest in you? Do you have to analyze everything to death? Get all the answers before you take any risks? No wonder you're not married."

Diana's head came up swiftly as fury arced through her. "Get out of here, Colby."

He stopped his pacing as the raw anger in her reached him. He grimaced. "Sorry," he muttered brusquely. "That was out of line."

"Yes, it was. I want you to leave. Now."

He ran his fingers through his hair again. "Look, forget I said that last bit, okay? I had no right."

"No right at all. Now leave before I sic my dog on you."

Specter growled obligingly and got to his feet. He watched Colby carefully, anticipation in every line of his massive body.

"Don't threaten me with your damn dog." Colby shot Specter a grim glance and then stalked toward Diana. "If you want to kick me out, do the job yourself."

"I'm trying."

Colby stopped a few steps away from her, regarding her with frustrated male anger and something else— something that might have been desperation. "I said I was sorry."

Diana raised her chin. "Why bother to apologize? I'm sure you meant every word."

"No, I didn't mean every word," he exploded. "Believe me, I sincerely regret every word. I wish I'd kept my mouth shut."

Diana walked to the door and opened it. "Good. Now please leave."

"Diana, wait. I want to talk to you."

"There's nothing left to talk about."

He moved slowly toward the open door. "I wonder if you're going to regret this as much as I will."

"Probably not," she said dryly. "I have nothing to regret."

"Lucky you." He strode past her, out into the night.

Diana closed the door behind him and leaned back against it. Outside in the yard the engine of Colby's black Jeep roared to life. Diana listened to it for a moment. Then she drew a deep, steadying breath and looked at Specter.

"I think," she said to the dog, "that I may have just made one of the biggest mistakes of my life. Either that or I had an extremely close call."

Specter came and leaned against her, offering silent comfort. Diana stroked his fur with an unsteady hand. "He scares me sometimes, Specter. But he fascinates me, too. I can't shake the feeling that I know him from some other place or some other time. Part of me says he's dangerous, but I can't figure out how I know that. And why do I have this strange feeling that he needs me? Worse yet, why do I need him?"

2

SCARLET MIST AND THUNDERING red water roared past him. The waterfall had turned to blood.

High above him yawned the black depths of the cave. Hidden in its deep shadows lay the entrance to the small grotto. The wrenching sense of longing and desperation that lapped at him in painful waves originated in that secret place.

He was working his way up the path behind the falls, knowing he would not be free until he had satisfied whatever lured him from within the cave. He could not leave until he had done what was required. But he also knew he could not do it alone. He needed her, but she must come to him willingly this time or they would both be trapped forever.

Colby snapped awake, shuddering as the last of the dream fragment faded. It was getting worse. He'd had the dream many times during the past twenty years, but it had never been as intense, as real and disturbing as it was this summer.

He sat up and swung his legs over the side of the bed. He started to switch on the lamp and changed his mind at the last instant. He didn't need light to show him that his hands were shaking. He could feel the faint shivers in his palms.

Annoyed, he got to his feet and padded, naked, downstairs to the old-fashioned kitchen. He opened the aging refrigerator, and stood contemplating its contents in the weak glow of the appliance light.

He had his choice of leftover tuna salad, sliced cheese, or pickles and beer. He chose the tuna and the beer. Closing the refrigerator door, he carried the bowl and the bottle over to the scarred oak table where he had eaten his haphazard meals as a boy.

Aunt Jesse hadn't been into cooking, either for herself or for the small nephew who had landed on her doorstep after the death of his mother. She'd been far more interested in her doomed career as a poet. Colby had learned early to keep food stocked in the refrigerator. If he forgot to do the grocery shopping, he and Jesse didn't eat.

Looking back he realized the kitchen experience had been good, practical preparation for the future. He owed Jesse for that much, at least.

Now, at forty, it was easier for him to feel a certain sympathy for Aunt Jesse's eccentric ways, her poet's ravaged temperament, her tendency to wallow in long bouts of depression and her desire for privacy. She had never wanted or needed anyone else, but she'd been stuck with Colby.

His hands were steady again. With a quick, practiced movement, Colby opened the bottle of beer. He took a long swallow of the brew and thought about how badly he'd screwed up earlier that evening.

He'd probably gotten exactly what he deserved.

What the hell had happened to him during the past few weeks? He'd been unable to get Diana Prentice out of his mind. She'd been haunting him in almost the same way the dream fragments had. But he'd figured he could do something about Diana, even if he was helpless against the dream. He could take Diana to bed and satisfy his obsession with her.

But tonight he'd gone too far. He'd blundered uncontrollably through the delicate spider web of a situation, and the whole thing had disintegrated in an instant.

He'd behaved like an idiot.

But what was done, was done. Colby was used to putting his mistakes behind him. Lord knew he'd had enough practice. The problem now was to figure out a way to recover all the ground he'd lost by trying to jump on Diana tonight.

Because somehow he had to find a way to make her see him again.

"YOU WANT THE WINDSHIELD WASHED, Miss Prentice?"

Diana smiled through the dusty glass at the lanky young man dressed in jungle fatigues. Eddy Spooner waited, poised with a rubber-bladed squeegee.

"Please, Eddy. It needs it."

"You bet. One thing we get plenty of around here during the summer is dust. You waiting for Colby to hit the post office?"

Diana's smile turned wry. Apparently everyone in Fulbrook Corners knew she and Colby had been dating. "That's right. Have you seen him yet this morning?"

"Nope." Spooner squinted past the pumps toward the small post office building on the opposite side of the main street. "No sign of him yet. You're a little early."

"Yes," Diana admitted softly, "I am." She'd driven into town early this morning precisely because she hadn't wanted to miss Colby when he showed up to collect his mail.

Diana considered the post office neutral ground. It seemed safer to try reestablishing the lines of communication with Colby there where they had first met, rather than taking the risk of going to the old, decaying house where he was staying.

Spooner stared at her through the windshield as he slowly raked the squeegee across the glass. Spooner did everything with a lethargic lack of interest. "You and Colby are hittin' it off pretty good, I hear."

"Really?" Diana made the response very cool. The last thing she wanted to do was talk about her relationship with Colby. Especially to a gas station attendant.

"It figures Colby would take a crack at the first classy broad we've seen around Fulbrook Corners in a month of Sundays. He always did go for the fancy ones. Folks said he had no business aimin' as high as he did. But I always told him—what the hell, go for it, man. What do you have to lose? Me and him used to spend a lot of time talkin' about women."

Diana took a closer look at the man who had been filling her gas tank once a week for the past few weeks. For the first time, she realized that Eddy Spooner was about Colby's age, maybe a year or two older. It struck her that these two men must have been contemporaries while they were growing up here in Fulbrook Corners.

That realization came as a surprise. Eddy Spooner looked as if he came from a different world than the one Colby inhabited. It wasn't just the jungle fatigues and heavy old military-style boots Spooner wore that gave that impression. Nor was it the thinning blond hair that fell to his collar. It was something else, something to do with the expression of lingering bitterness that marked what had probably once been a handsome face.

Spooner was the kind of man who would spend a lifetime blaming others and an unkind universe for everything that went wrong in his world. He looked like a man who'd seen a lot of dreams go up in smoke.

"You and Colby were friends as kids?" she ventured.

"Sure. Me and him used to hang out together. Sort of lost track of him after he left town. I spent a few years in the army and then came back here. But Colby, he lucked out. He didn't come back until this summer. Wonder why he bothered to now? He never did think much of this town and after what he did, most people in town sure don't think much of him."

Diana started to ask another question. Her curiosity about Colby was running rampant again. But before she could open her mouth, the familiar growl of a Jeep's engine caught her attention.

"There he is now. Looks like you timed things just right." Spooner dropped the squeegee into a bucket and came around to Diana's window. "Ten bucks even for the gas."

"Thanks, Eddy." Diana reached for her purse, one eye on the black Jeep that was coming to a halt outside the post office.

Spooner took the money and stared at Specter, who was sitting in the passenger seat watching attentively.

"That's sure some dog you got there."

Specter yawned, showing a lot of teeth. He was used to such observations.

"He's a comfort to have around at times," Diana murmured, patting Specter's shoulder.

"Yeah, a lady livin' alone needs a dog. I used to have me a dog. Real nice Shepherd. But he died a couple years back." Spooner turned his head to watch another car, an aging blue Cadillac, pull into the post office parking lot.

"I'd better be on my way," Diana said, turning the key in the ignition.

"If I was you, I wouldn't go rushin' into the post office just yet," Eddy advised. "Not unless you want to wind up in the middle of a real mess." There was a twisted smile on his face, as if he was taking a perverse pleasure in a secret knowledge of whatever was about to happen.

"Is something wrong?" Diana asked bluntly.

"Probably. See that big blue Caddy that just pulled up out front?"

"Yes." Colby had disappeared into the post office. Apparently he hadn't noticed her car parked across the street yet. Or if he had, he was choosing to ignore it. This was not going to be easy.

"See that old lady gettin' out of the Caddy?"

"What about her?" Diana asked impatiently. She briefly switched her gaze to the aging, gray-haired woman with the regal bearing who was getting slowly out of the passenger side of the Cadillac. She was being assisted by her driver, a large, beefy man of about forty-five whose potbelly strained the buttons of his shirt.

"That's Mrs. Fulbrook herself. Fulbrooks have owned just about everything in this town ever since my great grandpa's time."

"Is that right?"

Spooner must have sensed her lack of interest. He flattened one greasy palm on the roof of Diana's Buick and leaned down to look at her through squinted eyes. "You don't know nothin' about the high and mighty Mrs. Margaret Fulbrook, do you?"

"What should I know about her?"

"Well, for starters," Spooner said, drawing it out as slowly as he could, "She's Colby Savagar's mother-in-law."

"His mother-in-law!"

"Yup. And I'll tell you somethin' else. She hates his guts." Spooner stepped away from the car, apparently satisfied that he'd finally gotten her full attention. "See you next week, Miss Prentice. Nice talkin' to ya."

"Goodbye, Eddy." Diana pulled away from the gas station feeling dazed. Colby's mother-in-law? But Colby wasn't married.

She was *sure* he wasn't married. He couldn't be married.

He would have told her if he'd had a wife. Colby Savagar wouldn't play that kind of game.

But there was a lot she didn't know about Colby Savagar, Diana reminded herself as she parked her Buick next to Colby's Jeep. It was precisely that lack of knowledge that had kept her from going to bed with him last night.

She turned off the ignition and slipped out of the car. A small voice was urging her to turn around and drive away from what promised to be an unpleasant little scene. But the need to know the facts proved a far stronger motivation.

"Stay here, fella," she advised Specter. "I'll yell if I need help."

Specter was busy exchanging cold stares with the man who had driven the Cadillac. Diana took one glance at the overweight driver and then looked away. The man's heavily jowled face was marked with the cruel, not overly intelligent lines of a natural bully. Diana was willing to bet that this was the kind of man who had amused himself as a child by tearing wings off flies. She hurried toward the post office.

The tension in the lobby hit her like a tidal wave when she pushed open the glass doors. The silence was unnatural. Several people stood as if nailed to the floor. Instead of exchanging gossip and observations on the weather as usual, they were all mute, all staring with rapt attention at the scene that was unfolding before them.

Colby was just turning away from the counter, a bunch of mail in his fist. He glanced toward the door and saw Diana. For an instant he fixed her with his brilliant gray eyes, but a second later he jerked his attention back to Margaret Fulbrook who had planted herself directly in his path.

"Harry told me you'd come back this summer, Colby Savagar." Mrs. Fulbrook's voice had the carrying power of a woman who'd spent a lifetime commanding others and the situation around her. She wore her nearly seventy years with icy, rigid pride. Her hair was anchored in a queenly bun and her fine brown eyes were piercing. "I was inclined not to believe it at first. But then I recalled that the one thing you never lacked was the devil's own nerve."

Colby gave the older woman a chilling look. "Sometimes nerve was all I had. Excuse me, Mrs. Fulbrook. Someone's waiting for me."

"Who? That Prentice woman? I pity her. I've heard about her, too. Does she know what kind of man you are?"

"No, but then, neither do you," Colby said with soft savagery.

"You bastard," Mrs. Fulbrook hissed.

"You aren't the first to suggest that possibility and you probably won't be the last. But you sure can't say that about my son, can you? In fact, if I ever hear you say anything at all about my son, I'll . . ."

"Good morning, Colby." Diana unstuck herself from the floor and went forward with her best corporate smile, just as if she hadn't overheard a word. "I wondered if I'd see you here today. I was going to give you a call later and remind you about that trip to the falls you promised me." She switched her smile to the postal clerk behind the counter who was watching the confrontation with a gaping mouth. "Got anything for me today, Bernice? I'm in a hurry."

Bernice closed her mouth, her eyes darting from Colby to Mrs. Fulbrook to Diana. "Just this one letter." She handed it over the counter.

"Thanks." Diana took a quick glance at the familiar masculine scrawl and then dropped the envelope into her purse. She took Colby's arm in a casual gesture, aware of the battle-ready tension in his muscles. Then she smiled at the grim-faced Margaret Fulbrook. "You'll excuse us, won't you? Colby has been promising me this little outing for days. I've packed a lunch and everything."

"You're as big a fool as my daughter was. But at least you're no young, innocent girl. You look old enough to make your own mistakes. And mark my words, any woman who gets involved with Colby Savagar is making a serious mistake." Mrs. Fulbrook turned and swept disdainfully out of the lobby.

Instinct compelled Diana to urge Colby along in the other woman's wake. It was difficult to stage an exit if your intended victims did not take it seriously. Diana wanted to make certain no one in the post office assumed Colby was taking this scene to heart.

"It's going to be hot today," Diana remarked chattily as she crowded Colby through the swinging doors. "I was thinking of taking a swimming suit along on our picnic. Oh, and I'd better pick up some chips at the store. What's a picnic without potato chips? Have you got a cooler we can use?"

She fell silent as they stepped out into the bright morning warmth. The man in the Cadillac got out with ponderous slowness to assist Margaret Fulbrook into the passenger seat. When he threw Colby a vicious glare, Diana steered her charge in the opposite direction.

"Okay," Colby said quietly as they reached his black Jeep. "The rescue operation is over." He leaned against the fender and tapped his bunch of letters against one palm. "Should I thank you?"

Diana shaded her eyes and watched the Cadillac pull out of the parking lot. "I suppose that depends on how badly you wanted rescuing."

"Badly enough. It's been twenty years since I've gone toe-to-toe with that old bat. I'm out of practice. But I think I could still take Harry if I had to. He's really put on the weight. Looks slower than ever."

"Harry being the driver, I take it?"

"Harry Gedge being Margaret Fulbrook's odd job boy. He does whatever she tells him." Colby lost interest in the pair. "Were you serious about the picnic or was that just camouflage for the rescue effort?"

Diana drew in her breath and braced herself. "That depends on whether or not Margaret Fulbrook really is your mother-in-law."

Colby's brows rose sardonically. "Somebody sure filled you in fast."

"It was Eddy Spooner at the gas station," Diana admitted.

"Good old Eddy. Well, he was partly right. I married Margaret Fulbrook's daughter twenty years ago." He shifted his gaze to the disappearing Cadillac.

"Well?" Diana prompted.

"Well, what?" Colby looked back at her.

Diana sighed. "Are you still married?"

"No."

Diana hid her sense of relief behind a reproving shake of her head. "If I waited to get answers from you, I'd wait until hell froze over, wouldn't I?"

He smiled faintly. "And you like answers, don't you?"

"I need a few before I go to bed with you," she retorted evenly.

Colby didn't move. His expression was alive with sudden, searching intent. "Are you still considering the possibility of going to bed with me?"

"Yes."

Exultant relief flashed in his gray eyes, but he only nodded once. "If you come through with a real picnic this afternoon, I'll come through with some answers about Margaret Fulbrook."

"It's a deal." Diana turned to start toward her car.

"I'll pick you up in an hour. And wear a pair of sport shoes," Colby called after her. "It's slippery up there around the falls."

"I ACTED LIKE AN ASS last night. You have my apology, for what it's worth." Colby stretched out on his side with unconscious masculine grace. One knee was bent, his upper body braced on his elbow. His brooding gaze was on the town far below.

Diana was sitting cross-legged on the blanket, listening to the dull roar of the water. She followed Colby's gaze and studied the picturesque scene below. The road that paralleled the river through the gorge was a narrow, twisting ribbon. She could see the old bridge across the river that linked the two halves of Fulbrook Corners. Her cottage was just barely visible on the same side of the river as Colby's place.

Specter, having given up on the possibility of getting any more potato chips, was sprawled behind her on a sun-warmed rock.

"Maybe you did act like an ass," she agreed after a moment. "But part of it may have been my fault. I didn't handle the situation very well. I did a lot of thinking last night after you left. I've come to the conclusion you're right. I have been giving out mixed signals."

Colby's eyes shifted slowly from the scene in the valley below to her face. "Signals?"

Diana fiddled with a small weed she had picked. "Yes, signals. You know what I mean."

"I know what you mean, all right," he agreed roughly. "If nothing else, it's a relief to know I wasn't imagining things."

Diana's mouth curved in gentle amusement. "I expect that with an imagination like yours you have to be a little cautious about how you interpret things."

Colby picked up his beer can and took a long swallow. His eyes met hers over the rim. "I can control my imagination. Most of the time."

"I see. It's your hormones you have trouble controlling?"

His eyes gleamed in the sunlight. "I can control those most of the time, too. But around you they seem to go a little crazy."

Diana gnawed briefly on her lower lip and then opted for total honesty. "I think a part of me was thrilled to know that," she admitted very softly. "Because I was having the same kind of trouble controlling my, uh, raging hormones around you." She looked away, unable to meet his steady gaze. "I don't have that kind of problem normally. It's been a very long time since I felt on the edge the way I do around you."

"So maybe we should take pity on ourselves," Colby said dryly. "Let's go to bed together and work it out of our systems."

Diana gave a disgusted exclamation and leaned back on her elbows. "You're such a flaming romantic," she complained sarcastically.

"I write horror, not romance."

"That's no excuse," she snapped.

"It's time both of us stopped behaving like a couple of teenagers and started acting our ages. Neither of us needs a repeat of last night."

"I'll make another deal with you," Diana said. "If you don't mention last night again, neither will I."

Colby shrugged. "Whatever you want, so long as you're not trying to put an end to whatever it is we have going between us. Any more potato chips?"

"I think Specter ate the last of them."

"Figures." Colby threw a disgruntled glance at the sleeping dog. "One of these days, that monster and I are going to have a serious talk."

"Speaking of a serious talk . . ."

"Yeah?"

"Tell me about Margaret Fulbrook."

"I did promise you a few answers, didn't I?"

"Yes, you did."

Colby took another swallow of beer. "There's not all that much to tell. I was married to Cynthia Fulbrook. Technically, that made the old battle-ax my mother-in-law."

"What happened to Cynthia?"

"She died."

"Oh. I'm sorry."

"Margaret Fulbrook has always blamed me for Cynthia's death, among other things." Colby's mouth tightened. "I should probably take this from the top."

"I'm listening."

He drew a breath and shifted his eyes back to the little town below the falls. "My mother and my Aunt Jesse were both born in Fulbrook Corners. They came from the wrong side of the falls, as folks around here like to say." He smiled grimly and indicated a handful of rooftops on the left-hand side of the river. "They were stuck here all of their lives. My mother worked in a local café and dreamed of marrying some man from the other side of the river."

"And your Aunt Jesse?"

Colby's eyes softened slightly. "Aunt Jesse dreamed a lot, too, but not about marrying and moving to the right side of town. She poured out her dreams in an endless stream of poems and short stories that almost never got published. She considered herself a writer, even if no one else did, and she felt obliged to live up to the image. She was eccentric, unpredictable and erratic. She seemed to be in another world most of the time. But after Mom died, she didn't hesitate to take me in. Aunt Jesse was good to me in her own strange way. And she taught me things."

"What things?"

"How to take care of myself, mainly. She did it by leaving me to my own devices most of the time. It worked. I grew up knowing the only person you can count on is yourself."

"What about your father?" Diana asked cautiously.

"What about him? I sure as hell never had the privilege of meeting him. He worked for a lumber mill near here for a while—just long enough to get my mother pregnant—and then he took off."

"Oh."

Colby looked at her. "Yeah, that's about all you say about it. Oh. At any rate, to make an excruciatingly long, boring story short, I grew up with Aunt Jesse. And I guess I ran a little wild. I was the dangerous young hood from the other side of the falls. Always in trouble. Always blamed when there were missing hubcaps. Always the one people pointed at when there was a fight at the school dance. Always the one who got picked up when Sheriff Thorp heard about a midnight drag race out on River Road."

"And you were always perfectly innocent, of course?"

His lips twitched with a small smile. "Of course— except when it came to drag racing on River Road."

"In short, the kind of boy our mothers warned us about," Diana replied with a flash of amusement.

"Afraid so." Colby rolled onto his back and cradled his head on his folded arms.

"Well, that makes sense," Diana said calmly. "That was always the most interesting kind of boy, naturally. I always wanted to meet one."

Colby blinked lazily. "But you never did?"

"Unfortunately, no. I was never the type boys like that found fascinating. I wasn't very pretty for one thing, and I was much too serious for another. From my first day in school, I knew I had to make something of myself. I always had my head in a book. By the time I was out of high school, I was on the fast track to college and a career."

"And the kind of boy who swiped hubcaps, drove too fast and wore his hair too long wasn't interesting any more, was he? That kind of guy wouldn't have had any place in your up-and-coming life-style."

Diana refused to let him bait her. "I don't know if he would have fit in or not. I told you, I never got a chance to meet him."

"Be grateful. You might have wound up pregnant at eighteen, the way Cynthia Fulbrook did."

Diana hesitated a moment, absorbing that information. "You got Margaret Fulbrook's daughter pregnant?"

"Yeah."

Diana became irritated. "Well? Don't just stop there. How did it happen?"

He gave her an odd look. "The usual way."

"Colby, stop it. You know perfectly well what I mean."

He exhaled slowly. "Cynthia Fulbrook was the princess of Fulbrook Corners. She was the richest kid in town, the prettiest girl and the best-dressed student at Fulbrook Corners High. She got a brand-new red convertible from her parents the day she turned sixteen, and she had her choice of any boy in school. She was a year younger than me and I'd been as dazzled by her as every other male in town."

"How did she feel about you?"

"She found me *interesting*. But her parents kept a close watch on her."

"Ah, the old forbidden fruit syndrome."

"On both sides," Colby admitted. "But nothing happened between us until after I went into the service. I saw the army as a way out of Fulbrook Corners, and I took it the day I got out of high school. Eddy Spooner went with me. The summer of my nineteenth year I came home on leave and there was Cynthia, just graduated and getting ready to go off to college. She took one look at me and decided to find out what forbidden fruit tasted like."

"And you took one look at her and decided to see what it was like to go to bed with a genuine princess?"

"That's about it. But neither one of us were quite as grown up as we thought we were. I thought I knew all about taking precautions, and Cynthia thought she knew all about safe times of the month and other mythical means of avoiding pregnancy. The net result was that we took some chances we shouldn't have taken."

"And Cynthia got pregnant."

Colby nodded grimly. "There was hell to pay. Cynthia was scared to death. Her mother was screaming at her, and her father was threatening to have me put in jail or shot. They both agreed the pregnancy should be taken care of as quickly and quietly as possible. The last option anyone considered was allowing Cynthia to marry me and have the baby."

"So you ran off with her," Diana concluded.

"We thought we were in love. Or at least, I did. I also thought I had to protect her from her parents. I don't think poor Cynthia was thinking at all. She was a nervous wreck, torn between angry parents and the guy from the wrong side of the falls. I took charge, packed her up and drove her out of town before she had a chance to reconsider. We got married in Reno, and then I took her to the army base where I was stationed. She had Brandon seven months later."

"Brandon?"

"My son."

Diana smiled at the quiet pride in his voice. "What happened to Cynthia?"

Colby tossed a handful of pebbles out over the falls. "Cynthia's parents decided they could force her to come home if they threatened to cut off her inheritance. They never let up the pressure. And Cynthia did not take well to motherhood. She hadn't wanted Brandon in the first place. The whole thing had been a stupid accident, and she decided she shouldn't have to pay for it the rest of her life. Maybe she was right. Hell, I don't know."

"Who does at that age?"

"Yeah. Who knows? Cynthia and I fought a lot, and one day I came home to find her gone. She'd left a note for me telling me Brandon was at a neighbor's and that she couldn't take it any more. Her life had been ruined. She was going home to her parents. She wanted to start over. I never saw her again. She was killed in a freeway smashup on the interstate. Her parents never forgave me. At the funeral they told me they never wanted to see me or Brandon again. I was happy to grant them their wish."

"And you never married again?"

Colby shook his head. "I figured I'd seen enough of marriage to last me a lifetime. Besides, I was busy with my son. I raised Brandon by myself. Made a lot of mistakes along the way, but the kid turned out okay." Colby's eyes warmed with paternal satisfaction. "He just finished his first year in college in Eugene. Did great, too. Thinks he wants to be an engineer."

"Congratulations," Diana said softly. She folded her elbows on her drawn-up knees and rested her chin on her forearms. "It must have been rough at times."

Colby grimaced. "You don't know the half of it. Like I said, I made a lot of mistakes. Sure as hell wouldn't want to go through it again. But Brandon and I both survived."

"And that's the great saga of Colby Savagar and the town of Fulbrook Corners?"

He looked at her. "That's it."

"I think I understand why you haven't bothered to return before now."

Colby's intent gaze never left her face. "I answered your questions."

Diana felt the warmth in her face. She glanced away. "Yes, you did."

"I've got a few for you, too," Colby said quietly.

Pleased that he was finally showing some real interest in her background, she glanced at him. "You do?"

"Most of them can wait."

"Oh." She was strangely disappointed.

"All except one." Colby reached out and gently tumbled her down across his chest. "And that one is a very straightforward question. All it takes is a simple yes or no to answer it."

Instinctively Diana struggled to find her balance, but she didn't pull away once she had braced herself. She sprawled on top of him, her face very close to his.

"Yes or no, Diana?"

The roar of the falls filled her ears and the warm fragrance of the sun-heated woods enveloped her. Gossamer plumes of mist, creatures of light and magic soared overhead. One of her jeaned legs slid between Colby's thighs and got caught there. His body was strong and hard and infinitely inviting. His eyes were pools of gray fire waiting to blaze.

Diana realized with blinding clarity that she was falling in love.

"Yes," she whispered and lowered her head to kiss him.

3

HE HAD NEVER FELT so pulsatingly alive in his life. He was going to go up in flames at any moment. The blood beat heavily in his veins, and the ache in his loins was almost painful.

Colby held on to the woman in his arms with all his strength, afraid she would try to slip away from him again the way she had slipped away every other time he'd tried to make her his.

But this time she wasn't fighting him. This time she wasn't trying to edge out of reach. She was giving herself to him and his head spun with the wonder of it. All the hot, fierce questions his body had been asking would finally have answers.

"*Diana.* Honey, I've wanted you like this for so long. I've been going out of my mind."

She opened her mouth for him and he tasted her, whetting his own appetite even further. He cradled her legs between his own, anchoring her firmly against him. Then he slipped his hands under her shirt and traced the graceful line of her spine. She was supple and warm and very, very feminine. Colby groaned as desire raked him across hot coals.

He tugged the buttons of her shirt, pushing the garment off her shoulders with quick, impatient hands. Then he found the fastener of her bra and undid it. Her soft, gently curving breasts filled his palms and he lifted his hips, deliberately arching into her softness. Her skin was sleek and silky to the touch. He would never get enough of the feel of her.

"Colby, Colby, please. Yes, oh, please, just like that. You make me feel so good."

Captivated by her response, Colby grazed his palms again across her nipples. Tight, firm pebbles of desire formed beneath his hands. Touching was no longer enough. He lifted her higher along his chest until he could take the peak of one breast into his mouth.

"Yes," she breathed. A shiver went through her.

Colby tightened his hold on her and used his tongue to elicit another of the tantalizing little shudders of desire. The fact that he could make her react so fiercely only served to better fuel the fire that was burning within him.

She was scrabbling at his clothes now, unfastening buttons and pushing the denim shirt out of her way. Her fingers were as unsteady as his own. Her hands splayed across his chest, tangling in the rough hair there. When she lowered her head and touched the tip of her tongue to one of his own flat nipples, Colby groaned heavily.

He found the snap of her jeans and yanked at it. Then he fumbled with the zipper until he could slide his hand inside her flimsy panties. He snagged his fingers in the silky fabric that hid her secrets.

Diana writhed against him, crying out softly. He explored further and sucked in his breath when he felt the warm dew between her legs.

"Sweetheart," he muttered. "You want me. Say it. Tell me all about it." He probed gently with the tip of his thumb and her fingers clutched at his shoulders.

"I want you."

"Look at me," he urged, pushing carefully into her once more. "Open your eyes and say it."

Her long lashes swept up, revealing the gold and green and blue of her eyes. "I want you so much, Colby. I've never felt like this before in my life."

Her honesty almost shattered him. "It's the same for me," he admitted harshly. "I want you more than I've ever wanted anything in this world."

He pushed the jeans down over her hips and rolled her onto her back. Then he knelt, unbuckled his belt, and kicked himself free of his own denims. He hesitated a moment as she looked at him. An unfamiliar uncertainty flared briefly. He desperately wanted her to be satisfied. He wanted to please her. Then he saw the deep, feminine admiration in her eyes, and a sense of exultant relief rolled through his veins. *She was pleased with what she saw.*

"You're magnificent." Her eyes were glowing with soft, tremulous wonder.

"So are you." He drew his hand down the length of her from breast to thigh. "So are you," he repeated. "Oh, God, honey, you're perfect. Soft, sweet, beautiful. Perfect."

He parted her legs with his own and started to lower himself onto her. At the last instant a flicker of rationality went through his dazzled brain. He remembered the little foil packet he had optimistically put in his pocket before leaving the house.

"Just a second," he said hoarsely.

She nodded her understanding. He leaned down to give her a quick, hard kiss and then he reached for his jeans.

He took care of the small, crucial task with quick, efficient movements. Then he reached out to gather Diana back into his arms.

"Colby? I want you to know that I . . ."

He touched her mouth with his fingertips. "The last thing I want to do now is talk. I want you so much that unless we hurry this up, I'm going to explode before I ever get inside you. My self-control is shot to hell."

"Good," she said simply, mischief in her beautiful eyes. "I'm not in the mood for self-control either. Not now. Make love to me, Colby. Make it the way you said it would be the first time for us. Hot and wild and frantic."

He was enraptured by the siren song of her demand. And he was shaking with the effort it took to hold himself in check long enough to get himself into position. Then he was poised at the hot, damp core of her and he didn't have to wait any longer.

With a harsh exclamation of need, Colby drove himself into her soft, receptive core. He felt her quick, indrawn breath and the shudder that went through her. She was hot and tight. For an instant he feared his swift possession had hurt her. Her nails scored his shoulders.

Then she was clinging to him as if he were a lifeline, lifting herself to meet his demanding thrusts.

"*Colby.*"

And the first time with her was just as he had known it would be. Hot, wild, frantic.

Perfect.

"YOU'RE A SCREAMER."

Diana raised her lashes halfway, aware of the hot

sunlight filtering down through the trees and the heavy weight of Colby's leg as it lay across her bare thigh. "I did scream, didn't I?" she said, half-amused, half-bemused.

Colby raised himself on one elbow and grinned down at her. "Louder than Chained Lady Falls."

"Don't exaggerate. And don't look so damned pleased with yourself. Under certain circumstances, it could be highly embarrassing."

"It wouldn't ever embarrass me."

"Uh-huh. What if we'd been in a motel room or something?"

"What have you done in the past?"

"About the screaming?" She frowned slightly. "It's never been a problem."

"You don't spend a lot of time in motel rooms?" he asked innocently.

"I've never screamed before," she said quite seriously. She was not altogether certain she liked remembering that unmistakable evidence of sensual surrender. She was accustomed to being in control.

"Better get used to it," Colby advised. His eyes were brilliant with masculine satisfaction and anticipation. "You're going to be doing a lot of screaming in the near future."

"I am?"

He stroked a hand across her breasts and then bent over her. "Yes," he said softly. "You are."

"Colby?"

"Hmmm?" His arm tightened around her shoulders as he emitted a huge yawn.

"It's getting late. Won't be long until the sun sets. Maybe we should start back."

"We'll wait a little while longer. I want to show you something."

"The falls at sunset?" Diana sat up and picked up her shirt. The heat of the day was fading rapidly. "You said something about the water turning the color of blood. To be perfectly truthful, it doesn't sound all that terrific."

"You'll see. Where's that damned dog of yours?" Colby sat up and reached for his jeans.

Diana's glance got caught for a moment as she watched the smooth play of muscles under his skin. The strength in him was captivating. She had responded to it with more passion than she'd ever experienced. Colby saw her lingering look, and started to grin with lazy, come-hither sensuality. Diana quickly shifted her gaze to the woods, searching for her dog.

"Specter? Here, boy. Where are you? Specter? Over here, boy."

A soft, answering whine came from the trees. Diana smiled as the animal materialized from the woods. He appeared decidedly reproving. "Look at him. He probably wonders if we're finished acting like a couple of humans."

Colby chuckled. "I think we embarrassed him."

"I wouldn't be surprised. Specter has a great sense of dignity."

"Unlike you when you're going up in flames in my arms." Colby gave her a lingering kiss. "But it was good, lady. And I have a feeling it's going to get better and better." He got to his feet and tugged her up beside him. "Hurry up and get dressed. That sun will be in just the right position in another minute or two."

He helped her with the buttons of her shirt, and then she stepped quickly into her jeans and running shoes.

"Here we go. This is the best place to see the effect." Colby led her quickly to an outcropping of granite that gave a clear view of the thundering water. The mist boiled up into the air and settled lightly on Diana's tangled hair.

She looked down as the fading sun began to paint the sky. "It's beautiful," she said in surprise, as first the mist and then the cascading water turned a vivid gold. "I thought it would be red."

"Watch." Colby leaned forward intently, one foot braced on a chunk of rock.

Diana glanced at him curiously, wondering at his fascination. "You must have seen this hundreds of times."

"I used to come up here nearly every evening during the summer months when I was a kid." He didn't look at her. His whole attention was on the waterfall. "There. It's happening. See it? Like blood pouring out of the mountain."

Diana felt a distinct chill down her spine as she obeyed him and turned her gaze back to the falls. "My God, you're right," she whispered. "It's unbelievable."

"It's the blood of a dying warrior."

She wanted to ask him what he meant, but now wasn't the time. She stared in amazement, as fascinated as Colby was. The gold mist gradually shaded to orange and then to deep scarlet red. The effect lasted only a moment or two, and then the sun disappeared behind the mountains. The waterfall returned to its normal silver and white. Diana and Colby stood in silence for a moment. Then Colby reached out to hook an arm around her shoulders.

"Interesting, isn't it?" he asked a little too casually.

"It's weird," Diana retorted with feeling.

Colby laughed softly. "Yeah. Weird. Did I tell you there's a cave behind the falls? You can't see it because of the water, but if you know your way around down there, you can get to it."

"A cave?"

"Chained Lady Cave."

Diana leaned down to pick up the remnants of their picnic lunch. "How did the falls and the cave get that name? Chained Lady. It's strange."

"It's from an old legend." Colby folded the blanket and started to lead the way down the steep path to where the Jeep was parked.

"An Indian legend?"

He shook his head. "The Indians told it to the first settlers in the area, but they always swore the legend had nothing to do with their tribe. They claimed there was another race here before them. A fierce warrior people who had long since vanished."

"And the legend dates from that time?"

"Right."

"Tell me the story." Pebbles clattered under her feet as Diana hurried to keep up with him. She was suddenly keen to hear the tale of Chained Lady Falls.

"The way I heard it when I was a kid was that the warriors who inhabited this area had a habit of acquiring their wives through the time-honored procedure of kidnapping them."

"They sound like a typical bunch of male chauvinists."

"Don't look at me like that," Colby said with a sardonic glance over his shoulder. "I haven't kidnapped a woman in years. At any rate, it seems that one of the greatest of the clan's warriors decided he deserved the best. He wanted a woman who could give him a strong son. He hunted far and wide before he made his selection. Then he swooped down and grabbed the young lady one day while she was out picking berries. He carried her home and proudly installed her in his bed. But he'd made a slight miscalculation."

"The lady didn't like being kidnapped and carried away from her home and family?"

"She took strong exception to the whole situation. Under normal circumstances, her feelings on the subject would have been disregarded by all concerned. But in her case, her new husband couldn't totally overlook her opinion because she came from a very unusual clan. One in which the women were warriors. Not only that, but the females of the clan had learned how to control their reproductive cycles."

"Aha. In other words, she knew something about birth control and she refused to get pregnant. Good for her."

"Wait until you hear the end of the story before you start applauding."

Diana frowned at his back. "Is it going to have a happy ending?"

"No, it's not. Listen well, my sweet, and learn that female stubbornness doesn't pay off in the long run."

"Spoken like a modern-day chauvinist warrior type," Diana muttered.

Colby ignored her. "When several months of nightly effort on the part of our valiant warrior did not pay off, he finally realized his new bride was deliberately sabotaging his big plans to produce a mighty son and heir."

"And he was annoyed?"

"To put it mildly. He tried the usual beatings and threats, and when that didn't work, he decided the lady would come to her senses if she spent a little time alone in the cave behind the falls."

Diana's eyes widened. "He chained her in that cave you told me about?"

Colby nodded. "So the story goes." He leaped lightly down to another rocky ledge and had to dodge Specter who was bounding down the hillside ahead of him. "Out of my way, you dumb dog," Colby muttered through his teeth. Specter paid no attention.

"Stop maligning my dog, and tell me the rest of the story," Diana demanded.

Colby reached back to steady her. "Well, he stuck her in the cave and told her that she could come out only when she conceived."

"How awful."

"Every day just before sunset he came to her. He brought her food and made love to her and then he left her to face the darkness alone."

"You mean he raped her on a daily basis!"

Colby's eyebrows rose thoughtfully. "Yeah, that's probably what it amounted to, because the lady still refused to allow herself to become pregnant. And after a time she even refused to eat the food he brought her. All the while she was plotting, trying to figure out a way to get rid of her unwanted husband. One evening she saw her chance."

Diana looked up. "A chance to escape?"

"No," Colby said grimly. "A way to kill the warrior. She set a trap for him by pretending to surrender. He was so relieved to think he'd finally quelled her stubborn resistance that he apparently forgot just what kind of female he was dealing with. In his haste to get started on making a son, he got careless. Inexcusably careless, considering he was supposed to be a hotshot warrior."

"What happened?"

"The lady got hold of his hunting knife and she used it on him just as he was, uh, reaching the grand finale."

"She stabbed him to death while he was forcing himself on her," Diana concluded in awed wonder. "What a woman..."

"This story isn't over yet," Colby warned. "I told you that it doesn't have a happy ending."

"Finish it," Diana urged, anxious to hear the conclusion.

"The warrior died at her feet, his blood running out of the cave entrance and mingling with the waterfall. With his last breath, he cursed the woman. Told her that her spirit would remain chained in the cave forever until a child was conceived and born there."

"Then he croaked, and she managed to get out of the cave?" Diana demanded.

"She was still chained, don't forget. She had no way to get free after she'd killed the warrior. She died there, and the legend says her spirit is still trapped in the cave. After all, what are the odds that a baby is going to be created and born in Chained Lady Cave?"

"Pretty poor, I imagine." Diana glanced back at the impenetrable veil of the falls, trying to envision a hidden cave behind the wall of rushing water. It made her uneasy even to imagine it. "So that's the end of the story?"

"More or less. But for as long as I can remember, kids from around these parts have always had a lot of fun scaring each other to death with rumors that the Chained Lady is still waiting inside the cave. They say she'll kill any other male who dares to enter. The theory is that she's still got her husband's knife, you see."

"What do the adults say?"

"For the most part they laugh the whole thing off, naturally. But whenever something strange or unsettling happens anywhere in the vicinity of Fulbrook Corners, you can bet someone's likely to blame it on the restless spirit of the lady in the cave."

"I can see you were one of those kids who got off on that story," Diana said with a rueful amusement. She paused. "Tell me something. Did you ever risk going into the cave?"

He flashed her an unreadable glance. "What do you think?"

She tilted her head to one side, considering the question. "Oh, I think you probably did. You wouldn't have been able to resist the challenge. After all, you were the toughest kid in town, right? You had a reputation to protect."

Colby's smile was ironic. "You're right. I spent a night in Chained Lady Cave once when I was in my teens. Eddy Spooner and I were supposed to do it together on a dare. But when evening came and the falls turned red, Spooner lost his nerve. He opted to spend the night at a campsite down by the river."

"But you stayed, of course."

"Had to," Colby said with patently false modesty. "Like you said, I had a reputation to protect." His smile came and went.

"Were you terrified?"

The smile vanished. "I'll tell you the truth. I've never told any other living soul, not even Eddy Spooner. I've never been as scared in my life as I was that night. The only other time that I even came close to being that terrified was the night Brandon ran a fever of a hundred and five, and I had to rush him to emergency. But even that fear was a different kind than what I experienced in Chained Lady Cave."

The quiet forcefulness of that confession startled Diana. She had the feeling she had just looked through a window into a very dark, very private corner of Colby's soul.

"Colby?"

But he had reached the flat terrain at the base of the falls where the Jeep was parked, and he had turned his attention to other matters. "Look at that idiot dog of yours," he said in disgust as he strode toward the vehicle. "Sitting right up there in the front seat as if he owned it. Talk about nerve."

"Love me, love my dog," Diana said lightly, unthinkingly. It wasn't until Colby glanced back at her with a level, searching expression that she realized just what she'd said.

"Let's compromise," he said with a slow drawl. "I will *make love* to you. I will *tolerate* your dog."

"Let's hope he's willing to go on tolerating you for a while longer. Specter is a very opinionated dog." Diana slipped into the Jeep, and pushed Specter into the back seat. The dog went willingly enough. She hoped the act of maneuvering the animal's large, furry body hid her faint flush.

How long would Colby want to continue making love to her? And how long would she fool herself into thinking that making love was close enough to the real thing to make the compromise worthwhile?

"Is this where you used to stage your midnight drag races?" Diana asked as Colby swung the Jeep out onto River Road.

"Yeah, this is it. I won a lot of cash out here."

Diana's brows drew together disapprovingly as she studied the narrow road that twisted and curved to follow the river. "But this would be a very dangerous road to drive at high speeds. If a car went out of control around some of these curves, it would wind up in the river."

"Diana, my sweet innocent, I hate to break this to you, but the fact that the road is a little treacherous is what made the racing exciting. It's also why I won most of the time. No one knew this road as well as I did. I made a scientific study of every curve and straightaway."

"Somehow I can just imagine you doing that."

"I knew exactly how fast I could go into every turn and when to start accelerating on the way out. The races always started about a mile from here and finished at the falls. If I hadn't managed to shake the competition by the time I reached that hairpin turn in the road near the bridge, I almost always lost them at the curve near the falls."

"Your teenage years were certainly a lot more exciting than mine were," Diana murmured. "But I don't want you to go to the trouble of recreating them for me. Mind slowing down a little?"

Colby flashed her an apologetic glance. "Sorry." He eased off the Jeep's accelerator. "Does my driving bother you?"

"Not really," she said honestly. "You always seem to be in complete control." That much was true. Colby drove with a smooth precision that struck her as unusual. "It's just that I'm accustomed to a slightly more sedate pace."

"You want sedate—you get sedate." He grinned at her. "This evening your wish is my command."

"So accommodating... Amazing what a little sex will do for a man's mood."

"The little sex we had this afternoon was the best I've ever had, lady."

Diana blushed warmly, aware of the lingering aftershocks that were still rippling through her. She'd flown into a whirlwind and survived but she didn't think she would ever be the same again.

Specter sat with his head hanging over Colby's shoulder for the entire drive back to Diana's cottage. The dog's tongue lolled between his teeth and moisture dripped from it in a steady stream. By the time the Jeep pulled into the small driveway, there was a large, wet patch on Colby's denim shirt.

"You know," Diana said, examining the wet shirt, "I think it may be a sign that he's beginning to accept you."

Colby glowered at the dog who stared back with an astonishingly innocent expression. "No, Diana, it's not a sign that he's beginning to accept me. It's a sign that he's getting sneakier about showing how much he hates my guts. He knows he's losing the battle so he's going underground to engage in guerrilla warfare."

"You're getting paranoid."

"I believe in never underestimating the enemy." He loped up the porch steps and opened the cabin door. "Going to invite me in for dinner?"

She laughed. "Has it occurred to you that you may be turning into as big a mooch as my dog?"

"Specter only loves you because you know how to open a can of dog food. I, on the other hand, not only like your cooking, limited though your repertoire may be, but I'm crazy about your body."

"Where does my fascinating mind come into all this?"

"Honey, two out of three ain't bad. I'm certainly not complaining."

"You chauvinistic turkey." She punched him playfully in the ribs and had the satisfaction of seeing him double up in exaggerated pain. "You want dinner here tonight? You can cook it."

"Getting tired of doing all the cooking, hmm? I was afraid it would come to this," Colby said with an air of resigned gloom. "I should never have let you seduce me this afternoon. I should have known that once you knew you had me well and truly hooked, you'd walk all over me, abuse me and generally take me for granted."

Diana stood on tiptoe and brushed her lips across his cheek. "Who," she asked softly, "seduced who this afternoon?"

"*Whom*," he corrected with a grin. "The question is who seduced *whom*. Pay attention. Us writers know all about grammar and stuff like that."

"I'm impressed, but that doesn't answer my question." Diana swept past him and switched on the light. If nothing else, the sensual encounter this afternoon had certainly put Colby Savagar into a playful mood. She realized she'd never seen him in quite this mood until now.

"Sorry. I forgot. What was the question?"

"Now you're avoiding it."

"Avoiding what?"

"The question."

"Speaking of questions, I've got one for you."

She paused at the kitchen door, aware that he had lingered behind her in the hallway. She glanced back curiously. Colby was eyeing the letter and envelope she'd left on the hall table beside the vase of flowers.

"What's your question?" Diana asked pointedly.

He looked up, much of the playfulness in his expression gone. "Who's Aaron Crown?" He gave the letter a flick that sent it skidding to the far end of the table.

"My boss," she said slowly. "Or, to be more accurate, my ex-boss."

Colby followed her into the kitchen. "Why's he writing to you?"

She shrugged, pretending to ignore the faint challenge in Colby's voice. She pulled a head of lettuce out of the refrigerator. "Two reasons, I suppose. One, because we've worked together for quite a while and we're friends, and two, because he wants me to come back to my old job at Carruthers and Yale as soon as possible."

"Doing that accounting stuff you were doing before you took a leave of absence?"

"Yes." Colby had not displayed much interest in her job. He had only a vague idea of what she did for a living and did not realize just how much her career meant to her. Perhaps he simply didn't care. "Let's see you put together a salad. I'll open some wine and pour us both a drink."

"I thought it was the man's job to open the wine and sit around watching while the woman washed vegetables."

"I'm giving you credit for being somewhat liberated." She maneuvered the corkscrew into the bottle.

Colby hoisted the lettuce, his gaze speculative. "You said you took a leave of absence from that job of yours because you didn't get the promotion you expected."

"That's right. I was going to resign outright, but Aaron convinced me to take some time off and think things over. He said I'd been working too hard for too many years."

"You never mentioned this Aaron Crown before."

"Didn't I?"

"No, Diana, you didn't. Stop playing games with me. I read the first couple of paragraphs of that letter out there in the hall. Crown is practically begging you to come back to work for him. Are you sure he isn't more than just your boss?"

Diana sat down in a kitchen chair and put her feet up on the chair across from her. She sipped her wine, patted Specter on the head and thought about Aaron Crown.

Good-looking in a corporate kind of way, well-dressed in a corporate kind of way, congenial in a corporate kind of way, Aaron Crown should have been able to go very far in the corporate empire of Carruthers and Yale. And he certainly had risen fast enough when he had Diana Prentice around to make him look good. It would be interesting to see how well he did on his own.

"No," she said quietly. "Aaron has never been anything more than just my boss."

There was silence for a long moment as Colby tore lettuce. "I'm beginning to realize something," he said finally.

"What?"

"There's a lot I don't know about you."

Diana smiled into her wineglass. "You mean now that you've had your wicked way with me, you're finally getting curious about me?"

"First things first, I always say. I'm very good at establishing priorities and believe me, making love with you was number one on my list. Where do you keep the olive oil and vinegar?"

"Second cupboard on the right."

When Colby opened the wrong door, Specter came to attention and produced a warning growl.

"What the hell's the matter with him now?" Colby demanded.

"You've just opened the cupboard where I keep his dog food. Maybe he doesn't trust you around his food."

"Maybe he shouldn't trust me. We're enemies." Colby smiled slightly and closed the cupboard door. "The only thing I care about is whether or not *you* trust me. Do you, Diana?"

She sipped her wine and studied him. "I still don't know you very well."

"You're trying to sidestep the issue." He leaned back against the tiled counter and picked up the glass of wine she'd poured for him.

Diana took a deep breath. "I must trust you on some level, or I wouldn't have spent the afternoon doing what I did with you."

Colby nodded in satisfaction. "Yeah, that's the way I figured it, too." He turned back to the lettuce. "Did I ever tell you I make the world's best Caesar salad?"

"No, I don't believe you ever mentioned it."

"Wait until you've tasted it."

"Where did you learn to cook?" Diana asked curiously.

"From books. I had a kid to raise, remember? I decided I owed Brandon something besides frozen dinners and pizza, although he would have been just as happy with that level of cooking. I learned a lot of things about raising kids from books. I also found out the books aren't always right."

"No, I don't imagine they are. Did you want a child, Colby?"

"Not at the age of nineteen, I didn't," he said with an ironic twist of his mouth. "But I didn't have much choice in the matter. One fine day Brandon arrived and that settled it. There wasn't time to worry about whether or not I wanted a kid. I had one. What about you?"

The intimate question surprised her. Colby didn't ask such questions. Diana stared into her wine. She had wanted him to be curious about her, but not on this particular subject. She was not prepared to give him a full and complete answer, so she hedged with a portion of the truth. "I used to think about it sometimes. But somehow the right time and the right man never came together."

"Never?"

"Well, there was a man once, back when I was just starting my career. I was about twenty-five. I thought perhaps he might be the one. Things were very good for a while. But it turned out that he'd been on the rebound when he came into my life. When his ex-lover showed up, he realized that she was the one he really wanted."

"He walked out on you?"

"I've always been extremely grateful the ex-lover showed up before the wedding instead of after it," Diana said dryly. "At any rate, after that I quit thinking about a family and concentrated on building my career. Now I'm thirty-four and I'm content with what I have."

"You don't wonder what you missed?"

"Not really. Not often. I've built a full life based on a successful career, good friends and a variety of interests. I don't think I would have made a really terrific mother, anyway," she added with an attempt at lightening the unexpectedly tense atmosphere. "I've never been overwhelmed by the cuteness of kids and the thought of trying to get a child through the teenage years would traumatize me."

"It can be rough, all right. You get through it by doing what has to be done. But now that I'm a qualified expert, I'm more than happy to retire from the field. Raising kids is a job for starry-eyed people in their twenties who don't know what they're getting into."

"That I can believe." She stood up. "After thirty, you're old enough to be able to see what an undertaking it really is. At thirty-four, I'd be absolutely horrified at the prospect of getting pregnant."

Colby glanced at her with sudden understanding. "It would throw your whole carefully structured life into chaos, wouldn't it? It would change everything for you."

"Yes, frankly, it would," she shot back, miffed by his tone. "You sound as if you think it might be a good thing for me to have everything changed in my life."

Colby sliced a blood-red tomato into small chunks. "Yeah," he said. "Having a kid would definitely change everything for you."

"Well, that's one thing I don't have to worry about, do I?" she said very firmly.

"No," he agreed. "That's one thing you don't have to worry about. But maybe there are a few other, less drastic changes you could make in your life."

"Such as?"

"Such as moving in with me for the rest of the summer. Being the generous man that I am, I'm even willing to take your stupid dog."

4

HE HADN'T LIKED HER ANSWER but he'd handled it with his customary cool. Probably because he was convinced it wouldn't take him long to change her mind.

Suit yourself, he'd said. *No need to make a decision this minute. We'll talk about it some other time.*

Diana thought about Colby's implicit assumption for a long time after he'd left that night. He was probably right. She was already sleeping with him. Why not move in with him?

For the summer.

Deep inside, Diana knew that was the part that grated. Colby Savagar wasn't looking any further ahead than the end of the summer. He was certainly honest enough about that.

Restlessly, Diana pushed back the covers and left the bed. Specter got to his feet as she put on a robe and found her slippers. He looked up at her questioningly.

"Want a midnight snack?" Diana asked.

Specter's large, floppy ears snapped forward with eager attention, and he crowded close as Diana went down the hall.

"No need to ask you twice, is there? You and Colby both respond well to the stimulus of food."

Specter probably didn't care to be lumped together with his archrival but he kept quiet about it. He watched alertly as Diana dug out a dog biscuit and handed it to him. Specter took it from her fingers with great delicacy and then proceeded to swallow the snack in one chomp and a gulp.

"My, what big teeth you have," Diana said as she found a cracker for herself. "Colby's right. Those teeth do make a person wonder what you did for a living before you got this cushy job as my pal."

Specter grinned in what he probably felt was an engaging manner. Unfortunately the canine smile only succeeded in showing more teeth.

"Don't do that," Diana instructed firmly. "You remind me of Colby."

She sat down at the kitchen table to munch her cracker. The copy of *Shock Value* Colby had given her a few weeks earlier lay nearby. She was still trying to get the last paragraph of chapter ten out of her mind from yesterday's reading.

She hesitated a minute and then, unable to help herself, flipped the book open to find out what had happened to the main character, a man named Donnelly.

All he could think in those last seconds was that it wasn't right for a creature of such evil to appear in such innocent guise. A monster should look like a monster. A man should be able to tell the difference between good and evil at a glance.

But he had been too blind to see the truth and now the truth would kill him. Slowly, horribly, unmercifully, it would kill him.

Diana shuddered a little and quickly closed the book. She knew better than to read more of *Shock Value* at this time of night. She looked down at Specter.

"I think Donnelly's going to make it," she told the dog. "But we're all going to get our socks scared off in the process. Where do you suppose a writer of horror novels gets his ideas? I don't think I would want to dream Colby's dreams."

She got up and started to turn out the hall light. Aaron Crown's letter still lay on the small table near the door. Diana remembered Colby's reaction to it.

"The man spends one afternoon making love to me and he figures he's got a right to read my mail, Specter. Something tells me Colby's the possessive type. He's also arrogant, proud and capable of carrying a grudge against an entire town. I wonder why he came back to Fulbrook Corners this summer."

Specter gave her a look that clearly said, *who cares?* Then he yawned and padded down the hall to the bedroom.

COLBY LOOKED UP from the screen of the word processor and watched the morning sunlight fill the valley. In the distance Chained Lady Falls poured silver down the cliffs and Colby's body tightened as he remembered the events of the previous afternoon.

Making love to Diana had resulted in exactly the effect he'd half feared. It had deepened his need for her rather than slaked his thirst.

Why had she said no when he'd asked her to move in with him? They were already sleeping together. It seemed ridiculous not to share one house for the summer. He didn't think she was the type who would care what a townful of strangers thought about her living arrangements, but then, maybe she was.

There was a lot he didn't know about her yet. Colby was just beginning to realize how badly he wanted to know more, now that he had established the physical bond.

The compelling curiosity he was experiencing bothered him. In the first place, it wasn't like him. In the second place, she wasn't even his type. Diana was too self-contained, too confident of her own ability to take care of herself, too focused on her career. A regular twentieth-century amazon.

All in all, there was something about her that let him know she didn't really need a man in her life. A man had to work damned hard at convincing her he had his uses, even if only in bed. Diana was certainly different from every other woman he had ever known.

But in some ways he couldn't quite define, Colby sensed she was also a little like him—self-reliant, accustomed to making her own rules in life, opinionated. She would never expect anyone else to step in and clean up any mess in which she happened to find herself. She had obviously been taking care of herself for a long time.

There was an underlying feminine pride in her that he knew was ultimately bound to clash with his own masculine confidence.

But he had discovered to his profound satisfaction that he could make her shiver in his arms.

"Damn it to hell."

He was going to drive himself crazy if he kept thinking about her. He had a chapter to finish today. Colby punched the key that would save the paragraphs on the screen and then got to his feet. He'd been working since six. It was almost time to get the mail. If he got to the post office around ten-fifteen, he would probably run into Diana and they could have coffee together. Then they could make plans for the evening.

Twenty minutes later he grinned briefly to himself as he pulled into the small post office parking lot. Diana was already there. His smile faded as he remembered the letter she had collected yesterday. He hoped there wouldn't be another one from her boss. Colby had read enough in Crown's letter to know he didn't like the guy.

He didn't like any man who thought he could write to Diana in such friendly, familiar terms. The jerk had been pleading for Diana to come back to her old job, and there had been something in the tone of that plea that had really annoyed Colby. Aaron Crown had made it sound as if he had a claim on Diana, as if he had rights over her.

Colby vaulted from the Jeep and walked past Diana's sedate four-door Buick. Specter glared at him from the front seat.

"Forget it, you big ugly mutt, there's nothing you can do about it. I'm here to stay."

Specter growled just loud enough for Colby to hear.

"Hey, Savagar!"

Colby turned at the familiar voice. Eddy Spooner was hailing him from across the street. Colby waved a hand in acknowledgment. "Morning, Eddy. How's it going?"

Eddy glanced casually up and down the quiet street and then trotted across it. He was wearing his usual outfit, a faded pair of combat fatigues and heavy boots. He had a billed cap on his head and he was wiping his hands on an oily cloth. There was a hopeful smile on his face as he joined Colby.

"Can't complain," Eddy said. "Been waitin' for you to come into town this morning. How 'bout havin' that beer you and I talked about?"

Colby sighed inwardly but told himself he really couldn't put it off any longer. Twenty years was a long time but he couldn't ever forget that Spooner had once been the closest thing to a friend he'd ever had in Fulbrook Corners.

"Sure, Eddy. Sounds good."

"Come on out to the house this evening. I get off work at five."

The last thing Colby wanted to do was waste an evening drinking with Eddy Spooner. He had far more interesting plans for tonight. "Uh, I'm busy this evening, Eddy."

"That Prentice broad, huh? Can't say I blame you. She looks real slick. Real cool in those fancy clothes, but I bet she's probably a real hot piece of . . ."

"Don't say it, Spooner."

Spooner blinked at the blunt warning. Then his grin widened and he held up both hands in a placating gesture. "Okay, okay, I get the picture. No offense. So, when do you want to get together for the beer? We got a lot to talk about, old buddy. Tomorrow's my day off."

He'd better set a time and get it over with, Colby decided. "Right. Let's make it tomorrow. I work in the mornings. I'll come out to your place in the afternoon. I'll bring the beer. That work for you?"

"Sure, Colby. That'll work just fine," Spooner agreed happily. "See ya."

"Sure." Colby watched Spooner make his way back across the street. Everyone in town had said Eddy

Spooner wouldn't amount to much. They'd said the same thing about Colby Savagar.

They'd been wrong about Colby, and it looked like Eddy was at least managing to hold down a full-time job so maybe they'd been wrong about him, too. It was obvious Spooner wasn't drawing an executive salary, but he wasn't on welfare, either. Good for him.

Served the bastards right to be proven wrong. Neither Colby nor Spooner had wound up in jail or living on the streets despite all the predictions.

That kind of shared past produced a bond of sorts. He'd have that beer with Eddy Spooner. Maybe a couple of beers.

Diana was waiting for him inside the post office. She was just dropping a handful of letters into her big leather shoulder bag. Colby tried to see some of the return addresses, but he couldn't get a close enough look.

"Hi, honey," he said walking straight up to her and kissing her full on the mouth in front of Bernice and a cluster of post office patrons. "We've got to stop meeting like this."

Diana's cheeks turned a soft pink. She knew what he was doing. He was establishing a very obvious claim on her. If there was anyone left in town who wasn't aware that Colby Savagar was probably sleeping with that Portland woman who'd taken the Martin place for the summer, he would certainly know it by this afternoon. Colby was satisfied with the faint blush that bloomed in his victim's cheeks. He grinned.

"Hello, Colby," Diana said with deceptively bland politeness. "How are you this morning?"

"Take a guess," he invited, deliberately lacing the words with sensual satisfaction as he walked to the counter. "Hi, Bernice. Anything for me?"

"Right here, Colby." Bernice hastened to hand him a long white envelope that bore his agent's return address.

A check. Colby wondered if he'd ever get over the sense of amazed exhilaration he experienced when someone actually paid him real money for a book.

"You're in luck, Diana." Colby waved the envelope at her. "I think I can afford to feed you tonight." He started toward her with a wide grin and then halted abruptly as the post office doors swung inward, admitting two newcomers.

"Hi, Dad."

"*Brandon.*" Colby stared at the lean, dark-haired, brown-eyed young man in the doorway. His son was the last person he'd expected to see this morning. "What the hell are you doing here? You're supposed to be working in Portland."

Brandon Savagar moved a few steps into the room, his arm wrapped protectively around the shoulders of a strikingly pretty little blue-eyed redhead who looked about nineteen.

"Surprise," Brandon said with an almost aggressive cheerfulness. "There was a grease fire at the restaurant where I was working. Place is closed for two weeks. So I decided to come visit you. When I asked the guy at the station across the street for directions to the house, he said you were in here."

"Yeah. Sure. Good to see you." Colby realized Diana was looking at him with obvious interest. He recovered quickly and made the introductions. "Diana, this is my son, Brandon. Brandon, this is Diana Prentice. She's a, uh, friend of mine."

"How do you do, Miss Prentice?" Brandon said, exhibiting the manners Colby had drummed into him after reading a book on the importance of children learning proper social skills.

"It's a pleasure to meet you, Brandon," Diana responded gently.

Brandon glanced at his father. "Dad, this is a, uh, friend of mine. Robyn Lambert. Robyn, I'd like you to meet my father."

"I'm so excited to meet you, Mr. Savagar," Robyn said in a soft, shy voice. Her blue eyes were riveted on Colby. "I've read all your books. They're fabulous."

Colby looked at her, aware of the peculiar expression of determination in his son's eyes. His heart sank. A terrible premonition began to take shape. He fought it down. No need for panic. This was just another one of Brandon's girlfriends. At least the kid had good taste in literature.

"Hello, Robyn. I'm glad you like my books." He glanced at Diana and saw the laughter in her eyes.

"Congratulations, Robyn, you said exactly the right thing," Diana remarked. "I'm afraid that when I first met Colby, I didn't have the faintest idea who he was. I'd never read a horror novel in my life."

"She still hasn't," Colby put in. "She can't seem to get more than halfway through *Shock Value*."

Robyn looked astonished. "But that's one of his best."

"That's right," Brandon said seriously, his pride in his father very obvious. "*Shock Value* hit all the major bestseller lists. It was Dad's big breakthrough book."

"Enough," Diana cried. "I surrender. I admit I'm culturally illiterate when it comes to horror tales. I swear I'll finish the book, even if it scares me to death."

"Come on," Colby instructed, taking Diana's arm. "Let's get out of here. Brandon, you and Robyn can follow me out to Aunt Jesse's place. I'll be with you in a few minutes. I want to talk to Diana."

"Okay, Dad. We'll be in the car." Brandon nodded toward the sleek little two-seater Mazda Colby had bought for him when he'd gone off to college.

Colby frowned at Robyn Lambert's dancing red ponytail as the girl walked toward the car with Brandon.

"Only a nineteen-year-old looks that good in a pair of jeans," Diana said laconically. "But don't get any ideas. She's too young for you."

"You can say that again," Colby muttered. "Too young for Brandon, too. Or else he's too young for her. I'm not sure which."

"They both look about the same age."

"That's the whole problem. They're just kids." He leaned against the door on the driver's side of the Buick and wrapped his fingers lightly around Diana's forearms. "Now about tonight."

Specter immediately began to grumble menacingly. The dog leaned over to stick his nose through the open window, which put his teeth very close to Colby's thigh. Colby straightened quickly and stepped away from the car.

"Stupid dog."

Specter growled again, pleased at having made Colby move.

"Now don't you two start calling each other names," Diana admonished.

"Tell him that," Colby advised. "Listen, I wanted to invite myself over for dinner again tonight, but it looks like I've got company."

"Brandon looks a lot like you. Except for his eyes."

"He's got his mother's eyes," Colby said impatiently.

Diana snapped her fingers. "I knew they looked familiar. Margaret Fulbrook has those eyes."

"Probably. Honey, I don't want to talk about Brandon's eyes. As I said, I was going to invite myself to your place for dinner..."

"As usual?"

"Right. As usual. But now we'll have to change our plans."

"I wasn't aware we had plans."

"Diana, don't give me that wide-eyed, fuzz-brained look. It reminds me of your dog." Diana grinned and, exasperated, Colby bent his head to kiss the amusement from her soft mouth. "Now, then," he said a moment later. "As I was saying, we'll have to alter our plans. Come over to my place tonight. Brandon and I will fix dinner."

"Brandon knows how to cook?"

"Sure. I taught him how to read a cookbook."

Diana smiled quizzically. "You know something, Colby—I think you must have been a very good father."

"Sometimes the best thing you can say about being a father is that you survived and so did the kid. How about dinner tonight?"

"How can I resist letting you cook for me again?" She kissed him lightly. "I was very impressed last night. You were right about the Caesar salad. Best in the world."

"Told you so. See you at five. Leave the dog at home."

DIANA DID AS ORDERED and left Specter at the cottage. He had not been thrilled with the arrangement, and shortly after arriving at Colby's place, Diana, herself, had begun to question the wisdom of leaving the dog behind.

Specter made a great conversation piece, if nothing else, and it was obvious to Diana that the small party needed something to distract it. A definite tension was building between Colby and his son. Robyn Lambert seemed nervous.

"Perfect tacos," Diana said midway through the meal as conversation came to a halt. She tried a woman-to-woman smile on Robyn. "Men are so well suited to the kitchen, don't you think?"

Robyn blinked, her gaze uncertain as she looked at Brandon. "I don't know," she mumbled, nibbling on a tortilla chip.

Diana tried again. "Brandon, this salsa is just right. Hotter than a sidewalk in August. Did you make it, or did Colby?"

"Dad made it." Brandon gave her a small, uneasy smile and gallantly tried to follow her lead. "He likes it hot enough to set fire to the bowl."

"Brandon made the meat filling," Colby said quietly as he built another taco for himself. He took his time arranging layers of meat, cheese, lettuce, tomato and salsa. The words were his first in several long minutes.

"It's wonderful," Diana said quickly. "Some lucky woman is going to get a terrific husband. Imagine finding one who can cook."

Instantly she realized she had made a terrible faux pas. If the silence had weighed heavily on the table before, it was now crushing everything in sight. Robyn stared at her plate, her lower lip trembling. Brandon's expression was unaccountably grim. And Colby just sat at the head of the table taking savage chunks out of his taco.

Diana thought about getting up and leaving then and there. She wanted no part of a Savagar family quarrel. But something about Robyn Lambert's wounded blue eyes made her decide to stay. It wouldn't be fair to leave the poor girl alone here with Colby and his son if real trouble was brewing.

Without warning, Brandon set his glass of cola down hard on the table. "It's funny you should mention marriage, Miss Prentice," he said tightly. "The main reason Robyn and I are here is because we wanted to tell Dad we're thinking of getting married before going back to school in the fall."

No wonder Colby was sitting there looking as though he were about to explode. "I see," Diana said brightly. "How, uh, interesting." She could not think of anything else to say next.

"Dad doesn't think so," Brandon said.

Colby dropped the last of his unfinished taco onto his plate and fixed his son with a forbidding glare. "I think the idea is goddamned stupid, that's what I think."

Tears trembled in Robyn's eyes. Brandon's face hardened.

Diana winced. The gloves were off. She knew she and poor Robyn were about to witness a full-blown quarrel between the two men. "Excuse me," she said, rising swiftly. "I don't think I want to hear this. Robyn, would you like to come with me? Neither one of us needs to listen to these two do battle."

"Sit down," Colby said through his teeth.

"Give me one good reason," Diana invited.

Colby drew a deep breath, clearly making a superhuman effort to control himself. "Brandon and I will discuss the matter later. This isn't the time or the place."

"True." Diana sat down cautiously. "But I wasn't sure you realized it."

Brandon looked at her with respect. Apparently he wasn't accustomed to hearing his father handled in that manner. He hesitated nervously for a moment and then came up with what he undoubtedly assumed would be a safe topic of conversation.

"Dad said you were just here for the summer, Miss Prentice. How did you happen to pick Fulbrook Corners? From what Dad's told me and from what I've seen, this isn't exactly the vacation spot of the western hemisphere."

Diana took pity on him. She smiled slightly. "I'm not sure why I picked this little town. I took a leave of absence from my job in Portland, and I felt I had to get away from the city for a while. I wanted a complete change of scene. As I told Colby, I just got out a map and Fulbrook Corners caught my eye. It turned out there were a few cottages available, so I took one for the summer."

Brandon nodded. "How come you took a leave from your job?"

"Well, it's a complicated story. I was in line for a promotion at the manufacturing firm where I had been working for the past four years. I felt I deserved the promotion. I'd worked extremely hard for it and, to be honest, I thought it was in the bag."

"What kind of work do you do?" Brandon asked.

"I have a degree in accounting and one in business administration. I was working as second-in-command in the office of a division controller at Carruthers and Yale."

"So you did financial forecasting and things like that?"

Diana nodded, delighted by his interest. "That's right. I helped work up the forecasts and also did a lot of accounting administration work. It's all computerized these days, you know."

"So what happened to the big promotion?"

"As I said, I didn't get it. When it didn't come through, I was forced to reconsider my situation. It became apparent that women could advance to the ranks of middle management but no higher at Carruthers and Yale. The men at the top had drawn the line at the divisional level."

Robyn looked up, showing faint interest in the conversation. "You think you were denied the job because of sexual discrimination?"

"I have to assume that was the reason. There was no one else as qualified for the job as I was and everyone knew it."

"But that's illegal," Robyn said with a puzzled frown.

"I've got news for you, Robyn. Just because there are now laws in place to protect women from discrimination on the job doesn't mean it's always easy to get em-

ployers to obey them. In my case, I could never prove
discrimination and there was no real way to fight it."

"So you took a leave to think things over." Brandon
nodded understandingly. "Going to go back?"

"No. I've done a lot of thinking, and I'm sure I'll end
up resigning my position. You have to know when to
cut your losses in the corporate world," Diana explained calmly.

"But didn't the whole situation make you mad?"
Brandon persisted.

Diana looked up from her taco and for an instant all
the helpless fury she had experienced at the time was
mirrored in her eyes. "Oh, yes," she whispered tightly,
"it made me angry. More angry than I've ever been in
my entire life. Nor have I ever felt so frustrated and
helpless. I had worked hard for that promotion. I'd put
in countless hours of unpaid overtime. I had put out
one fire after another for my boss. When I first started
to work in the division, it was losing a half a million a
year. Within a year we were breaking even, and six
months later we were clearing a profit. That division
of Carruthers and Yale now makes a million and a half
a year. And I had a lot to do with the turnaround, damn
it."

"Oh, wow," Brandon said, looking rather awed.
Colby and Robyn were staring at her as if they hadn't
noticed her sitting there at the table until now.

"But where I really went wrong," Diana continued
with barely suppressed violence, "was believing the
upper management of Carruthers and Yale when it
claimed it would treat women equally on the job. I put
my faith in a bunch of male executives who lied through
their teeth. They used me, but when it came time to

promote me, they ignored me. Yes, Brandon, it made me angry."

Another taut silence descended on the table as the last of Diana's fury evaporated. She had her temper in hand almost immediately, but Colby was still looking at her with a stunned expression.

"Christ, Diana, I hadn't realized it had been like that for you," Colby said bluntly. "Why didn't you tell me how bad it was?"

She shrugged. "You never asked."

"No," he admitted slowly. "I didn't, did I?"

Robyn looked genuinely puzzled. "But I thought it was different for women now."

"Sometimes it is. Sometimes it isn't. Mostly it isn't. Not at the higher corporate levels."

Brandon spoke up. "How will you know if it's going to be any better at your next job?"

"Good question," Diana said, trying to lighten her voice. "It's one of the risks women face in the business world. The only way to know for sure it might be better would be to start my own business, I suppose." She looked at Robyn. "What type of career are you thinking of for yourself, Robyn?"

Robyn chewed her lip nervously and looked quickly at Brandon. "I'm not sure yet. I mean I haven't thought too much about it. It'll probably depend on what Brandon does. That is, I mean if we, uh—" She broke off abruptly.

"Surely you're not basing your career decisions on what Brandon does, or whether you get married," Diana said in genuine amazement. "Every woman has a responsibility to be able to take care of herself."

"You sound like one of those hard-line feminists we have to study in college," Robyn muttered.

"No," Diana said easily. "I'm just practical. I've seen enough of life and the world to know that when the chips are down the only one you can really count on is yourself. Right, Colby?"

Colby studied her intently. "Yeah. Right. Do you want another taco, Diana?"

She laughed and got up. "No thanks, I'm stuffed. That was a delicious meal. Seeing as how you and Brandon fixed the dinner, I think Robyn and I can handle the dishes. Okay with you, Robyn?"

Robyn nodded reluctantly. Diana got the impression she didn't want to be separated from Brandon by even a few feet. But she got up and began collecting dishes.

"This is a creepy old house, isn't it?" Robyn said as she followed Diana into the kitchen.

Diana looked around at the old two-story structure. The house was in decent repair, but there was an undeniable air of shabby gloom about it. The floorboards squeaked. The walls were bare. The appliances were old. The halls were dark. The furniture was ancient and worn-out, and the drapes were so faded that it was difficult to detect any sign of their original flower print.

There was something quietly, eerily sad about Aunt Jesse's old house, as if the woman's unfulfilled dreams still hovered there.

"Yes, it is a little creepy. Sort of fits the image of the kind of house a horror writer should live in, though," Diana said briskly.

Robyn gnawed on her lip again. "Mr. Savagar hates me."

"Don't be silly. He can't possibly hate you. He hardly knows you. It's the idea of you and Brandon getting married that he doesn't like. He feels you're both too young."

"Brandon said his father was married at nineteen."

"Which is precisely why he's bound to be opposed to Brandon marrying at the same age. He knows nineteen is too young to make that kind of commitment."

"You're on Mr. Savagar's side, aren't you?"

"Not exactly. I do have my own opinions on some things, though, and I'll admit I don't think a woman should consider marriage until she's established a career of her own. It's just too big a risk."

"You sound just like my parents. They're always telling me what I should do. Always trying to dictate my life. They think I'm still a child and they treat me like one."

"They probably just don't want you to make any serious mistakes at your age," Diana said soothingly, thinking that she was highly unqualified to be lecturing a teenager on how to conduct her life. She'd had absolutely zero experience in child-rearing.

"Brandon and I are adults, you know. We can make our own decisions."

"Part of being an adult is not feeling it's necessary to tell other adults that you are one."

"What's that supposed to mean?" Robyn appeared genuinely bewildered.

"Never mind."

"It's not as if the people who don't want us to get married know what they're talking about," Robyn continued earnestly. "Take yourself, for example. You're a lot older than me, you've got a career and everything and you've never married. Do you think I want to end up like you? And look at Mr. Savagar. He's not married either. My parents may be married, but they're always yelling at each other. Always fighting. The fact is, none of you know what real love is."

Diana saw the incipient tears in Robyn's eyes. She gave her a wry smile. "You may have a point, Robyn."

5

"COULDN'T WAIT TO GET OUT of there, could you?" Colby demanded roughly as he followed Diana into her cottage an hour later. He tossed her car keys down on the hall table. He had insisted on driving her home and intended to walk back to his place. "Can't blame you. I wish I could walk away from that mess myself."

"It's a common enough situation, Colby. Just a couple of young people in the throes of first love."

"A couple of young fools, you mean. Easy enough for you to sound calm. You're not the one who has to deal with it." He shoved his fingers through his hair. "Marriage. I can't believe it. After all I taught that kid. After all the lectures I gave him on not tying himself down to the first pretty face who comes along. Damn it, Diana, what the hell am I going to do?"

"I don't know," Diana said gently, pouring him a glass of brandy. Specter watched broodingly. She tossed him a dog biscuit.

"I can't let him do it. He'll ruin his whole life. He's got a great future waiting for him. The last thing he needs is to be saddled with a wife and maybe a couple of kids. I've got to make him see that. I can't let him make the same damned fool mistake I made."

"Stop pacing, Colby, you're making Specter nervous."

Colby swore under his breath and swallowed half the brandy in his glass. He looked at Diana mutely for a long moment. "I hadn't realized how upset you were about your situation at Carruthers and Yale."

She sipped her own brandy reflectively. "I'll find another job. I've got contacts in the business world. I've got a good track record. Something will turn up."

"You're cool enough about it now, but when Brandon brought up the subject at dinner, it was clear you'd been through hell. It really got to you. It was a major career disaster for you, wasn't it?"

"These things happen in business."

"Did that boss of yours—Aaron Crown—did he go to bat for you?"

"Aaron said he did everything he could for me. Gave me the highest possible recommendation. Tried to talk the powers that be into making good on their promise to deal fairly with a woman in management. But upper management was inflexible."

"And I'll bet you were as cool as a cucumber right through it all. No tears. No rage. No big emotional scenes and no recriminations."

"One of the first things a woman learns in business is that men do not respect, let alone understand, what they think of as typical female emotions. It's very important for a woman's business image that she never cry or lose her self-control around the men she works with or for."

"Maybe the management at Carruthers and Yale would have a little respect for someone's hands wrapped around their collective throats. I'd like to try it. Maybe I could convince them to be a little more flexible. They had no right to do that to you."

Specter growled, responding to the trace of genuine savagery in Colby's words.

"Thanks for the sympathy, guys," Diana said with a smile.

"Why didn't you explain just what had happened at Carruthers and Yale before?" Colby held up one palm before she could answer. "Never mind. You've already told me why. My own fault. I didn't ask."

"It's my problem. No reason you should be burdened with it."

He eyed her closely. "You're the most self-contained woman I've ever met, Diana."

"I don't think I'm any more self-contained than you are."

He considered that. "We've got a few things in common, I guess. He resumed his pacing. "Damn, I wish I could spend the night with you."

"Going back to your place to play chaperon?"

"Don't laugh at me. That's exactly what I'm going to do." Colby braced one hand against the wall and gulped the rest of the brandy. He stared out into the darkness. "Think he's sleeping with her?"

Diana was taken aback. "How would I know? You're his father and you're a man. What do you think?"

"I can't tell for sure. Maybe I don't want to know for certain. Hell, Diana, if he gets her pregnant, if he's as stupid about that kind of thing as I was at nineteen . . ."

"I assume that along with teaching Brandon how to cook and how to use good manners, you also taught him the facts of life and how to protect himself and a woman?"

"Are you kidding? I wasn't going to have him grow up believing the usual garbled batch of rumors, misconceptions and mythical nonsense a boy picks up from his buddies. I drilled the facts into him from the time he was old enough to understand that little girls were different."

"What kind of sleeping arrangements did they request?" Diana asked. "One bedroom or two?"

"I didn't give them a chance to make a request. I put them into separate bedrooms as soon as we got back to Aunt Jesse's."

Diana couldn't restrain a burst of delighted laughter. "Poor Colby. I'm sorry," she managed when he scowled at her. "I guess it's not really very funny from your point of view."

Colby came away from the wall in a smooth, lithe movement, set down his glass and reached out to draw her quickly to her feet. "You're right. It's not funny. Brandon is a kid of nineteen. He hasn't got a glimmer of what he's getting into." Colby paused thoughtfully. "Maybe I should try to talk him into living with her for a while before they make a decision on marriage. I have a hunch the charm of the idea would fade quickly once they started playing house."

"Easy for you to suggest. You're the father of the young man involved. The parents of the young woman involved may not like the idea of their daughter living with a man at all."

"Damn."

Diana smiled up into his thoroughly frustrated eyes. "I suppose you should be getting back to your place. The duties of a chaperon are quite demanding, I understand."

Colby swore again. Then he kissed her heavily. "Later," he promised in a husky voice as he reluctantly released her. "We'll finish this later."

Specter grinned a wide doggy grin as Colby stalked out the front door.

"SO, WHAT'S SHE LIKE?" Eddy Spooner asked after the second beer. "She any good in bed?"

"Get stuffed, Spooner. I didn't come here to talk about Diana. She's none of your business." Colby leaned back against the front porch steps and took a swallow of beer. He was already regretting his decision to drive out here this afternoon. The bonds of past friendship were looking weaker and less meaningful by the minute.

"Okay, okay, I was just askin'." Spooner concentrated on his beer for a while. "Maybe I'm just feeling a little envious, you know? Been a long time since I had me a woman. That Miss Prentice of yours is about the first really interesting female we've had in town in ten years. She looks classy but kind of chilly. Can't blame a guy for wonderin' what she's really like."

Colby didn't respond to that. Diana was anything but cold when she lay in his arms, but he sure as hell wasn't going to share that information with Eddy Spooner or anyone else. Colby considered everything about Diana his own personal turf. He was beginning to realize he didn't want any other man even coming close to her.

He rolled the cold beer can between his palms and stared out at the swaying fir trees that surrounded the old, ramshackle house. The Spooner place looked almost the same as it had twenty years ago, he reflected.

A general air of neglect still enveloped every inch of it. The front porch still sagged, and one window was boarded up. There wasn't a scrap of paint left on the wood. Eddy's father had always been too drunk most of the time to tend to home repairs.

Both front and back yards were still filled with weeds and the skeletal remains of old automobiles. Eddy's old Camaro was parked in front. The paint job on the car matched the design on Eddy's fatigues, but Colby knew the engine would be in perfect condition. Eddy's one great passion in life had been cars, Colby remembered.

"You ever marry, Eddy?"

Eddy closed his eyes and rested his head against a post. "Yeah. Girl I met right after I got out of the army. Her name was Angie. Lasted about a year. Then the bitch ran off with some dude from Seattle."

Colby nodded in silent commiseration. "Never tried it again, huh?"

"There was another one. A sexy little redhead. I thought she'd be okay. Had the wedding all set and everything. I was gonna move down to Portland and find a good job, you know. But just before the big day, I found out she was still sleepin' with an old boyfriend of hers. Figured there was no point tryin' again after that. Bitches are all the same."

"You like working at the gas station in town?"

Spooner shrugged. "It's a job. Nothin' else has ever worked out for me, not the way things worked out for you. Came close a time or two, but things fell apart."

"Close to what?" Colby glanced at him curiously.

"Close to gettin' a real break." Spooner stared at Colby through narrowed eyes. "Once, just after the army, I met a guy who had a line on something real hot. Something he'd set up during his tour in the Philippines. He was gonna cut me in on a piece of the action. But things folded."

"Tough." Colby wondered what the action had been, and decided it would be better not to ask.

"Then, another time, I thought I had something set with some dude who owned a string of massage parlors. I was gonna manage a couple of them for him. Sort of be a bouncer, you know? Except I was gonna get a piece of the business. But that didn't work out either. There were one or two other things but, like I said, nothin' ever worked out. Everything always went wrong."

"So you came back here. Never thought you'd wind up in Fulbrook Corners, Eddy. I thought you hated this town as much as I did."

"I still hate it," Spooner muttered. "But after Pa died, I owned this place free and clear, and Clark gave me that job down at the station. What was I supposed to do?"

"I don't know," Colby said honestly, hating the whine in Eddy's voice and simultaneously feeling guilty for his reaction. Eddy's life had been a hard one.

"Hell, you wouldn't understand. You got lucky. You weren't trapped here the way I was."

"No." Luck came in a variety of guises, Colby decided.

"You always came out on top." Eddy was silent for a moment. "Saw your kid in town today. Knew who he was the minute he drove into the station. He looks like you, but he's got those Fulbrook eyes, don't he?"

"Yeah. He's got Cynthia's eyes."

"You gonna introduce him to old lady Fulbrook?"

Colby's mouth twisted slightly. "Are you kidding? She met him once when he was a baby and told me she never wanted to see him again."

"Dumb question, I guess." Spooner paused to open another can of beer. "I read one of those books you wrote. *Shock* something or other."

Colby felt a flicker of surprise. "Did you? I didn't think you liked to read, Eddy."

"TV's more interestin' than books, usually, especially now that Sam's renting movies down at the grocery store. Got me a VCR and old Sam's got a few of them X-rated flicks he keeps behind the counter."

"I see. Old Sam sounds like he's decided to move with the times. What made you read *Shock Value*?"

"Dunno. Guess I was kind of curious about what you'd been up to. Everybody in town was talkin' about that *Shock* book when it came out. Reckon they couldn't believe it was you who wrote it. Bessie must have sold a hundred copies the first week it came into her shop. She said everyone in town wanted to read it. Maybe they was worried you'd put a couple of local folks in the story."

Colby couldn't suppress a certain grim satisfaction. "It was the first book of mine to hit some of the major bestseller lists."

"Make you rich?"

Colby grinned. "Not exactly, but I'll admit it sure changed a few things for me and Brandon."

"I always figured that of the two of us, you'd probably be the one who'd make out okay."

The bitter resignation in Spooner's voice bothered Colby. "It's not too late for you, Eddy. You've got no obligations. No wife and kids to tie you down. You're only forty-one. Why not get out of this town and try someplace else?"

"Sure. Doin' what, for instance?"

"You're a first-class mechanic. You always had a way with cars. You could get a job in Seattle or Portland or maybe somewhere in California. Good mechanics are always in demand, especially by people who own those foreign jobs. Hell, some of those folks would probably put you on a retainer just to keep their BMW or Mercedes running."

"I told you, Colby. I already tried to get out of here. Things always fall through. I never had the magic touch like you did."

"There was no magic touch, Eddy."

"Who are you trying to kid? You always got the breaks. I couldn't believe it when you actually talked Cynthia Fulbrook into marrying you. Richest, prettiest girl in town. Nobody could believe it. People talked about it for months after you and she left. Old Lady Fulbrook and her old man ranted and raved and cursed you up one side and down the other. Then old man Fulbrook croaked and we heard about Cynthia dying in that car crash. Old lady Fulbrook hasn't been quite the same since. Serves her right, the old bat. Always thinkin' Fulbrooks was so much better than everyone else."

Colby concentrated on an old tire that was lying in the front yard. He didn't want to think about Margaret Fulbrook. "When did your father die?"

"The year I finished my hitch in the army. Drunk as a skunk, as usual. Went out huntin' and fell off the top of Chained Lady Falls. No loss. To tell you the truth, I was kind of surprised he bothered to leave me this place. Course, who else did he have to leave it to?"

"That's a fact. You were his only kin." Colby remembered the bastard who had been Eddy's father. The man had been violent when he drank. Eddy had suffered from that violence frequently when he was younger.

However erratic life had been with Aunt Jesse, however emotionally neglected Colby had been while Jesse pursued her poetry, at least he'd never been subjected to physical violence the way Spooner had.

Eddy finished his beer. "You still hate this town as much as you used to?"

"Yeah," said Colby. "I still hate it."

"Why'd you come back?"

"I needed a place to finish the book I'm working on. And I decided it was time to get rid of Aunt Jesse's place. Too much trouble keeping it rented to summer tourists."

"Larry Brockton down at the real estate office said once that you'd given him instructions to keep the place fixed up and rented out during the summer."

"I didn't know what else to do with it after Aunt Jesse died."

"So you're here to take care of that old business and finish another one of them horror books, huh?"

"Right. I thought Fulbrook Corners might offer some inspiration for my writing," Colby explained dryly.

"Inspiration! Here? That's a laugh."

"It is, isn't it?"

"Come to think of it, Chained Lady Falls might be sort of inspirational for a horror writer," Spooner remarked slowly. "Remember that night we were gonna spend there?"

"I remember it."

"You never told anyone I didn't stay with you in that damned cave."

"No point."

"Guess I never thanked you for keepin' your mouth shut about that."

"Forget it, Eddy. That was a long time ago. It doesn't matter now."

"That's kind of what I figured. It doesn't matter much now. Nothing does."

DIANA STOOD STARING UP at Chained Lady Falls. The billowing mist dampened her hair as well as the oxford cloth shirt she was wearing with her khaki trousers. The rocks at the base of the falls were slippery. She'd almost fallen once or twice, trying to get close enough to see the hidden entrance to the cave. She still couldn't spot it through the thundering water.

And she still wasn't sure why she had driven out here to take another look at the falls this afternoon. Something about the place had drawn her back for another look. She peered upward, trying to envision a path behind the white veil. The cliff behind the falls looked sheer, offering no obvious footholds.

But Colby had said he and Eddy Spooner had climbed up to the cave the time they had dared each other to spend the night in it. There must be a path. She just couldn't see it.

The legend of Chained Lady Cave had begun to fascinate her. She'd awakened this morning thinking about it, and now she couldn't seem to stop.

At her side, Specter whined softly. Absently, Diana reached down to pat his mist-dampened coat. "What's the matter? Don't like getting wet, do you? You've never been real big on taking baths. Well, come along, then. I think we've seen enough."

Diana made her way carefully over the wet rocks toward the car. "I wonder if Colby would agree to show me the inside of that cave?"

She pondered her own curiosity all the way back to her cottage. It wasn't until Specter gave a sharp, warning bark as they pulled into the drive that she realized someone was sitting patiently on her front porch.

"Hello, Brandon. I didn't expect to see you here. How are you today?"

Brandon got to his feet and smiled tentatively. "Hi, Miss Prentice. I walked over to see you. Dad's gone to see an old buddy of his. Didn't know if you were gone for the day or what."

"I just went for a drive. Come on inside. I think I've got some beer in the refrigerator. And please call me Diana."

"Thanks. I could use a drink. It's hot today." He followed her into the house, idly patting Specter who was tolerant of the caress.

"My dog seems to like you. You should be flattered." In the kitchen Diana opened the refrigerator and found a can of beer. "He doesn't think much of your father, you know."

"Is that right?" Brandon looked surprised. "Dad's usually pretty good with animals. We always had pets around when I was growing up."

"For some reason Specter and Colby have agreed to disagree. They have their own private war going. I try to remain neutral." She handed Brandon the beer and poured herself a glass of iced tea. "Have a seat."

Brandon dropped into a kitchen chair, his casual sprawl reminiscent of his father's easy masculine grace. His young face was set in serious lines as he spent a few seconds groping for the right words. "I came by to ask a favor, Miss . . . I mean Diana. A big favor."

Diana's heart sank. "If this has anything to do with family matters, Brandon, I would prefer to stay out of it. After all, I'm just a friend of your father's."

Brandon's eyes widened. "You're more than a friend. I can tell by the way Dad looks at you." A dull red tinged his cheeks. He looked away. "Sorry. I didn't mean to be rude. It's just that I know he likes you. A lot. And, well, I thought maybe you could talk to him. God knows I can't."

"Have you tried?"

Brandon nodded wearily. "I tried again last night after Robyn went to bed. It was a disaster. We ended up yelling at each other. I've always been able to talk to him until now. But his mind is absolutely closed on the subject."

"He's got his reasons, Brandon."

Brandon grimaced. "He thinks history is going to repeat itself. He won't even listen to me. Heck, all I want to do is talk to him about it, you know? I want to explain about Robyn and her folks."

"What about Robyn and her folks?" Diana asked.

"They're always on her back. Always telling her what to do. They scream at each other, and then they scream at her. They won't let her do anything on her own."

"How did she get permission to come up here with you?"

Brandon's mouth tightened. "They think she's with a girlfriend on the coast."

"Oh, brother."

Brandon stared at her helplessly. "You see what I mean? I've got to talk to Dad. And fast. I want to ask him some questions. If I could just get him to be reasonable, maybe I could decide what to do."

"Brandon, I don't think anyone could get your father to be reasonable about something unless he wanted to be reasonable about it. And in this case, where he feels he's right, I suspect the chances of me being able to influence him are absolutely zero. I think your best bet is to just back off for a while. You and Robyn are going to be together at school next year, aren't you?"

"Yes."

"Well? It's not as if someone is going to pry the two of you apart. Why rush into marriage? Give it some time. Let your father see the relationship is solid and for real, if indeed it is solid and real."

Brandon looked down at the can in his hand. "Robyn doesn't want to wait. She wants to get married so that she can get away from her parents."

"What about you? What do you want to do?" Diana asked gently.

"I . . . care for her. A lot. I kind of feel sorry for her. If she wants to get married right away, then I guess that's okay with me."

"Are you sure, Brandon?"

He looked up, dark eyes almost fierce. "I'm sure!"

"All right. Calm down. I was just asking. The decision to marry is a very big one. Look at me, I was never able to make it," Diana quipped.

Brandon looked puzzled. "You've never married?"

"No."

"No kids?"

"No kids."

"Don't you want any?"

Diana laughed. "Even if I did, it's a little late to start having them now."

"That's not true. You're not that old," Brandon said with awkward gallantry. "You hear about those famous movie stars putting off having babies for years."

Diana grinned. "Thanks. Unfortunately, I'm not a famous movie star."

Brandon turned brick red. "I'm sorry, I didn't mean..."

"Forget it. I know what you meant, and it's very kind of you. Another beer?"

"No thanks." He paused. "Getting married wasn't the only thing Dad and I argued about last night."

"Oh?"

"I asked him about my grandmother. She lives here in Fulbrook Corners."

"Yes, I know. I saw her briefly in the post office the other day."

Brandon's head snapped up, his eyes alive with deep interest. "You did? You know her?"

Diana hesitated, beginning to realize she might have said too much. "No, not really. She was just, uh, pointed out to me."

"It's weird to have a grandmother you've never even met," Brandon said slowly. "I don't remember Aunt Jesse too well. She came to see us a couple of times when I was a kid. But then she died. All my life it's mostly just been me and Dad. Do you think my grandmother really hates me?"

"Is that what your father said?" Diana asked carefully.

"He said she doesn't want anything to do with me or him. She blames him for what happened to my mother."

Brandon stared at Diana with an intensity that reminded her of his father. When he reached forty, she reflected, this young man was going to be every bit as formidable as Colby Savagar.

"And you want to meet her? Is that it, Brandon?" Diana asked quietly.

He fiddled with the beer can. "I'd like to get a look at her. Find out what she's like. I guess I'm curious, that's all."

"I can understand that. Why not tell your father just that?"

"I tried last night. He was already mad because of Robyn. When I brought up the subject of my grandmother, he really went through the roof. Said he wasn't going to let the old bitch get near me."

Diana groaned. "Your father can be extremely opinionated."

Brandon's mouth curved wryly. "Yeah, I've told him that on several occasions. Once he makes up his mind, getting him to change it is like trying to move a mountain."

"I know what you mean." Diana thought of the intent way Colby had been pursuing her for the past few weeks. He had been unswerving. And she had eventually succumbed to the inevitable.

"I'm just curious. What's wrong with that?"

"Nothing. I'm sure your father thinks he's protecting you from what might be an unpleasant scene, that's all."

"I can handle it. He's taught me to handle things like unpleasant scenes. Heck, he even signed us both up for karate lessons when I was a kid. We practice together a lot. He ought to know I can handle meeting my grandmother."

"Maybe he's right about Margaret Fulbrook not wanting to meet you. I hate to point that out, Brandon, but it's something to consider. The woman is old and apparently very bitter. She might not be rational about the whole thing." Remembering Margaret Fulbrook's reaction to Colby in the post office, Diana was fairly certain the woman wasn't entirely rational about her son-in-law and grandson.

The growl of a Jeep engine cut off whatever Brandon might have said in reply. Specter surged to his feet with an answering growl.

"Must be your father," Diana said, half-amused. "Specter makes that particular noise only when Colby's in the vicinity."

"Damn." Brandon got hastily to his feet. "Excuse me—but I was hoping Dad wouldn't find out I'd been here. You won't tell him what I asked you to do, will you? He'll be furious if he thinks I dragged you into this and he's mad enough already."

Diana saw the anxious look in Brandon's eyes and took pity on him. "Don't worry," she assured him as she listened to Colby take the front steps two at a time, "I'll consider our conversation confidential."

"Thanks." Brandon looked enormously relieved. "Geez, your dog really doesn't like Dad at all, does he? Look at him."

Specter was bounding forward, toenails scrabbling on the wooden floor as he rounded the corner at a dead run and headed for the hall. He reached the front door just as it opened.

"Damned dog." Colby's irritation carried into the kitchen. "When in hell are you going to learn that I've got as much right to be here as you do? Out of my way, you mangy mutt. *Diana.*"

"In here, Colby."

She looked up with a smile as he strode into the kitchen, ignoring Specter who was making menacing sounds at his heels. Colby's eyes went instantly to hers, but then he caught sight of his son.

"What the devil are you doing here, Brandon?"

"He just came by to say hello," Diana said easily. "That's enough, Specter. You've made your point. Take it easy, boy. Go lie down. I can handle this."

Specter uttered one last final woof of disapproval before flopping down under the kitchen table. From his self-appointed den he kept a wary eye on Colby.

"One of these days that dog and I are going to have it out. Where's Robyn?" Colby opened the refrigerator with easy familiarity and helped himself to the iced tea.

"She's back at the house reading one of your books. She really loves your stuff, Dad." Brandon's voice was almost painfully eager.

Colby grunted and leaned back against the sink, his eyes on Diana. "Where did you go this afternoon?"

She flashed him a look of surprise. "How did you know I'd gone anywhere?"

"The hood of your car is warm. Engine's still hot." He tossed back the iced tea.

"Well, aren't you observant," Diana murmured. "Maybe you should be writing crime fiction instead of horror. As a matter of fact, I drove out to Chained Lady Falls."

"What for?"

She lifted one shoulder. "I don't know. I just wanted to get out for a while, and that seemed like an interesting place to drive to."

"Is that the falls you can see in the distance when you're driving into town?" Brandon asked.

Colby nodded. "You and Robyn can fix your own dinner tonight. Or go into town and eat at one of the cafés. Diana and I are going to be busy."

"Sure, Dad." Brandon got to his feet and dropped his empty can into the trash. "See you later, Diana. It was nice talking to you."

"Goodbye, Brandon. Thanks for stopping by."

Specter walked him to the door, tail wagging in a friendly fashion. Colby watched his son leave. When the front door slammed shut he turned to Diana.

"Let's have it. What was he doing here?"

Diana frowned. "I told you, Colby. He just dropped in to visit."

"Without the precious girlfriend in tow? Doesn't make sense. He must have wanted something. Did he want you to exercise the sweet voice of reason over me? Get me to see what a jewel sweet Robyn is and what a good idea it would be if the two of them got married?"

Colby obviously knew his son all too well. But Diana remembered her promise to Brandon. "Never mind what Brandon wanted. I want something."

He arched his brows. "What's that?"

She leaned one elbow on the table and rested her chin on her hand. "Colby, I'd like to see that cave behind Chained Lady Falls."

He was startled. "You want to go into the cave? Why?"

"I don't know. Curiosity, I suppose. Maybe I'm just getting bored sitting around here working on my résumé day after day. It seems to be one of the local sights, and I'm playing tourist this summer. Will you show it to me?"

6

"HOW THE HELL did you talk me into this? I should be working on my book this afternoon. I'm not even sure I can still find the path. Watch your step and stay right behind me." Colby mixed commands with a great deal of mild complaining as he prepared to lead Diana behind the roaring water.

"Yes, oh great leader. I hear and obey. And to be honest, I don't know how I did manage to talk you into this. Guess I must have caught you in a weak moment." Diana grinned up at him through the thick mist. A splash of water drenched the front of her shirt.

Colby's eyes gleamed. His gaze lingered on her damp shirt. The cotton cloth clung to her, outlining the soft swell of her breasts and their thrusting nipples.

"You forgot to wear a bra," he announced. "You look like an entrant in a wet T-shirt contest."

"You've attended a lot of wet T-shirt contests?" Diana asked with grave interest.

"You'd be surprised at the variety of programming available these days on the sports channel."

"I can imagine." She had assumed it would be easier to scramble over rocks without the binding encumbrance of a bra, but she had forgotten the predictable effect of the perpetual mist that surrounded Chained Lady Falls. "Are you sure there's really a path behind the water?"

"There was twenty years ago. A wide granite ledge. It should still be there. Put on your rain slicker. It's going to be wet on the other side of the waterfall." He shrugged into the waterproof windbreaker he'd brought along for himself. "At least we don't have to deal with that idiot dog of yours today."

"He didn't like being left behind at the cottage."

"He'll survive," Colby declared harshly. "And we sure don't need him underfoot on that ledge."

Diana unfastened her yellow slicker and adjusted the hood. After that there was almost no conversation except for an occasional shouted instruction from Colby. The roar of the water made it impossible to speak in normal tones.

Colby found the trail after a few minutes of trial and error. It was a surprisingly easy, if steep, climb to the cave halfway up the side of the cliff. Being behind the falls was an odd experience, however. Diana felt as if she'd stepped into another world.

The torrent created a great, impenetrable shield of noise and power and cut off the view of the valley and town below. The force of the pouring water was awesome. The rocky ledge seemed safe enough, but it occurred to her that if someone slipped and went over the side there would be little chance of surviving the fall.

They reached the yawning mouth of Chained Lady Cave about ten minutes later. Diana stepped through the entrance with a sense of relief. The climb up hadn't been too precarious, but the constant rush of water only inches away was disconcerting.

The cave was heavily shadowed but far from completely dark. Some of the bright sunlight outside managed to pass through the wall of water, illuminating the interior with a faint glow.

Colby switched on the flashlight he had slung on his belt and led the way several feet into the cavern. The farther they moved from the entrance, the darker the shadows grew. The noise of the falls faded somewhat, making conversation possible again.

Diana reached for the flashlight on her own belt, and stared at the damp cave walls. "So this is where he kept her chained. How ghastly."

Colby glanced at her. "Take it easy, honey. It's just a legend, remember?"

"In another hour the sun will be going down. I wonder what the water looks like from this side when it turns red."

"It looks like several tons of blood pouring straight down in front of your eyes."

"Your imagination is sometimes a little too vivid."

"Occupational hazard for a writer of horror fiction."

Diana glanced around. "Is this where you spent the night? On this wet floor?"

"No." Colby was walking toward the back of the cave.

"Where are you going?"

"Since I'm here, I thought I'd check and see if the place where I did spend the night still looks the same."

She followed curiously. "You mean there's more to the cave than just this one big room?"

"Uh-huh. Stay close. Remember I told you I was scared right down to my toes that night?"

"I remember."

"Well, I stumbled around, trying to find a reasonably dry place to sleep, and I eventually wandered into a really weird little grotto. The entrance is hidden way in the back of the main chamber. I only found it by accident. Wait until you see it."

"Colby, I don't know if I want to go any farther into this place."

"Stay out here in the main lobby, then. I'll just be a few minutes." He was edging along the cave wall, heading deeper into the inky darkness.

"Oh, no, you don't. I can do anything you can do."

"Atta girl."

Diana's chin lifted. "Don't be condescending."

"Sometimes you're too damn touchy, honey. Lighten up." Colby and the comforting beam of his flashlight vanished.

"Damn you, Colby Savagar." Diana hastened forward and flashed her own light into the deep shadows where he had disappeared. She could see nothing for a moment, and then she saw a section of darkness that was blacker than the shadows around it. Cautiously she stepped toward it. A moment later she found herself in a small, rocky antechamber.

"Take a look," Colby invited, as if showing off the Taj Mahal. "It's really something, isn't it?"

Her first impression was of warmth. A rocky pool filled a large portion of the room and the water in it was obviously very warm. Diana shone the beam of her light down into the depths of the pool and realized she couldn't see the bottom.

"This is where I spent the night," Colby said quietly. "And I never told Eddy Spooner or anyone else about this hidden room. As far as I know, no one else has ever found it."

"I think that warrior in the legend knew about it," Diana said with sudden conviction. "This is where he kept his poor wife. Not in the outer cavern."

Colby gave her an odd glance. "Know something? The night I spent in here, I was convinced that this was where she stabbed him. Somehow I just knew it."

"Why did you stay in here instead of in the main chamber?"

Colby played his flashlight beam on the walls. "Damned if I know. I just wandered in here and decided it was as good a place as any to spend the night. It was warm in here."

"But it's a lot creepier in here than it is out in the front part of the cave. If I had to choose, I'd sleep out there. Then again," Diana added wryly, "I doubt that I'd get any sleeping done at all if I had to spend the night in this place."

He was watching her through narrowed eyes, the harsh planes and angles of his face thrown into sharp relief by the back glow of the flashlight. "Do caves make you nervous?"

She started to shake her head, then stopped. "I suppose so. I've never spent much time in them. But it's more than that." She broke off.

"Go on," Colby urged softly.

"I don't know how to explain it," Diana admitted. "There's just something very strange about this particular grotto. A feeling."

"What kind of feeling?" he persisted.

Exasperated, she stepped back toward the entrance. "Stop it, Colby. Are you deliberately trying to frighten me?"

"No. I just want you to tell me exactly how you feel about this place."

He moved toward her, making no sound in his soft-soled shoes. He kept the flashlight pointed at her feet. His face was in shadow but his eyes seemed to gleam implacably in the darkness. He loomed over her—large, powerful, wholly male. She was suddenly aware of how vulnerable she was, here alone with him. If she screamed, no one would hear her.

Without any warning, Diana's imagination slipped into high gear. She no longer saw a reasonably civilized twentieth-century male, but a bronzed warrior. *The muscles of his broad shoulders were sleek and contoured from years of violence. She shuddered at the fierce strength in him and the utter determination that blazed in his eyes.*

He was a great leader, a skilled fighter, a lord among his people, and she belonged to him as completely as his war-horse or the lethal blade he wore at his belt.

He would take her. He thought he had the right to do so. He had been raised from birth to think he was entitled to anything he wanted. And now he wanted a son.

If he had come to her with gentleness, if he had treated her with the respect that was her due, if he had acknowledged her value as an equal, then perhaps, just perhaps, she would have given him willingly what he took by force.

But the warrior knew only the ways of male violence and she would never surrender to such ways. She would never give him a child to be raised in those ways.

There was no hope for either of them in this life. No chance to learn each other's hidden secrets, calm each other's private fears, trust in each other's strengths. No hope for love and gentleness and comfort.

There was no hope in this time and place.

But there would be other lifetimes.

"Diana? Are you all right?"

Diana blinked quickly, taking a frantic grasp on her wayward imagination and thoroughly ruffled nerves. Abruptly, she wanted nothing more than to get out of the grotto.

"What is it, honey?"

"Never mind how I feel about this place. I don't want to talk about it." She whirled to slip back through the opening in the wall, stumbling with relief into the main chamber.

Colby was right behind her. "Diana, what the hell's the matter with you? Are you sure you're okay?"

"Of course I'm okay. I just don't like that little grotto. Maybe your overactive imagination is rubbing off on me."

"Take it easy, honey." He came up behind her, putting a casually comforting arm around her shoulders.

She looked at him, seeing the affectionate amusement in his eyes and the slight curve of his hard mouth. The last traces of her conjured-up image of a warrior vanished. Colby was tough but he wasn't cold-blooded or violent. Smiling wryly, she leaned against him for a moment, seeking comfort from his lean, strong body. He nuzzled the spot behind her ear.

"I'm all right," she mumbled. "But I don't think I was cut out for this. I can't imagine how people can take this kind of thing up as a lifelong hobby. What do you think they get out of it?"

"The chance to comfort terrified lady friends?" He bit her earlobe gently.

"Colby, why is it so dark in here? Is the sun setting already?"

He lifted his head abruptly, glancing toward the cave entrance. It was far darker here in the outer chamber than it had been a few minutes ago when they had first entered. The faint rays of sunlight that had shone through the veil of water no longer filtered into the room.

"No, the sun isn't setting yet. Too early." Colby released her and walked toward the entrance with a frown. "The only thing that could make it get this dark so fast is a storm," he called back above the roar of water.

"A storm? But nothing like that was forecast, not even rain." She followed him to the cavern entrance and peered out. The wall of water falling in front of them had turned a deep steel gray.

"Stay here a minute," Colby shouted. "I want to see how bad it is out there." He stepped out onto the ledge and moved along the path to a point where he could see through the mist. Diana saw how the wind whipped his hair and the water drenched his windbreaker. He returned with a set expression on his face.

"What's wrong?" Diana demanded.

"It's storming out there, all right. Must have come up out of nowhere. A real mean summer thunderbuster. The water's coming down so hard, you can't tell where the waterfall ends and the rain begins. Wind's really howling, too. We'll have to wait until it lightens up before we try to go down that ledge."

"But the ledge is already wet from the mist of the falls. What harm will a little more water do?"

"It's not just the rain, it's the way the wind is driving it. If it caught you just right, it would be strong enough to make you lose your balance. Even if we got down the path in one piece, I'm not anxious to be walking behind that water when the lightning strikes."

As if to confirm his opinion, thunder crashed outside, louder than the falls, and an instant later a flash of light glittered on the other side of the cascade. The lightning faded instantly, leaving the pouring water darker than ever.

"You may have a point," Diana said reluctantly. She backed away from the entrance. "How long do you think it will last?"

"Shouldn't last too long. These summer storms are wicked but short-lived," Colby said easily. "Come on, let's find a place to sit down and wait it out." He guided her toward the back of the main chamber where it was easier to talk.

Colby seated himself on a convenient outcropping and arranged the flashlights so that they provided illumination without having to be held. Diana sank down beside him, aware of a chill from her damp feet.

"Since we're going to have to entertain each other for the next few minutes," Colby said smoothly, "why don't you tell me the real reason my son came to visit you today?"

She threw him a disgusted glance. "I hate nagging men."

Colby's gaze hardened. "He's my son, remember? I've got a right to know what's going on."

"Nothing's *going on*, as you put it." Diana shifted a little on the hard rock, trying to get comfortable. She stared out at the barrier of roaring black water.

"Now, listen, Diana . . ."

"Do you want some free, unsolicited advice, Colby?"

"No, damn it, I don't." He hesitated and then flung a handful of pebbles across the floor of the cave. "What advice?"

"If I were you, I wouldn't push Brandon very hard right now. You may force him into a decision he doesn't really want to make."

"He's already made a decision. Or thinks he has. I'm going to change his mind if it's the last thing I do." Colby hurled another fistful of pebbles.

"I don't think he's talked himself completely into marriage," Diana said thoughtfully. "I think he's being pushed into it by Robyn. He obviously cares for her. He's worried about her because of her relationship with her parents. And he's attracted to her. He wants to please her, but I don't think he really wants to marry her. At least, not at this stage."

Colby gave her a sharp look. "I agree little Robyn is probably pushing, but what makes you think Brandon's not eager?"

"He's a lot like you," Diana said simply.

"Too much like me, apparently. He's dead set on making the same mistakes I made at nineteen. But what the hell's that got to do with it?"

"Colby, that's not what I meant," she said patiently. "When Brandon showed up a couple of days ago, all he said was that he and Robyn were *thinking* of getting married."

"So?"

"So, is that the way you would have handled the announcement if you were determined to get married? Even at the tender age of nineteen, I'll bet once you'd made up your mind to marry Cynthia, you didn't announce it in such a wishy-washy fashion. My guess is that you just came right out and told everyone you were *going* to get married, like it or lump it. You wouldn't have stood around arguing about it, and you certainly wouldn't have worried too much about getting parental approval."

Colby stilled. His eyes gleamed reflectively. "You're right."

"As I said, I think your son is a lot like you. If he had been hell-bent on marriage, he would have announced the fact that he was going to marry, not that he was thinking about it and if he got any grief from you, he wouldn't have stuck around to argue. He and Robyn would be on their way to Reno by now."

Colby stared at her in silence for a few seconds. "So why is he sticking around trying to convince me he's ready for marriage?"

"Possibly because he's looking for a way to get out of the situation and doesn't know how to do it without hurting the woman he cares so much about. He feels trapped. His instincts undoubtedly sent him to you because he's hoping you'll help him figure a way out. You're his father and he's learned a lot from you over the years. He respects you. But yelling at him that he can't possibly marry Robyn won't work. It's the wrong approach."

"Why not? If he wants an out, let him tell her his father won't approve the marriage."

Diana sighed. "And be forced to admit to himself and to Robyn that at the grown-up age of nineteen he can't do anything without his father's permission? Come on, Colby. You know what a male ego is. You've got one yourself."

Colby swore softly. He leaned back against the damp cavern wall, drew up one leg and draped his arm over his knee. He glowered at Diana.

"This is getting complicated," he said.

She gave him a tiny smile. "Not really. Just think it through logically. I have a hunch your son has gotten himself in an awkward bind. He likes Robyn but he isn't ready to marry anyone, and deep down he knows it."

"What's he want from me?"

"What he came up here to do was talk to you. He wants the benefit of your wisdom, logic and experience so he can use it to pick a path through the brambles that surround him. But he doesn't want to be yelled at. He doesn't want to be forced to admit that you can still tell him what to do. Push him into a corner, and he'll dig in and show you just how independent he is."

"You mean, keep yelling at him and he'll marry Robyn just to show me he can make his own decisions."

"That's the way it looks to me," Diana said softly. "I may be wrong. You certainly know him better than I do. But I definitely get the feeling he isn't all that enthusiastic about marriage."

"And if I calm down and stop yelling at him, I might be able to help him figure out how to get out of the situation? You may be right, Diana. It makes a certain kind of sense. The trouble is, I'm not sure I can stay cool and rational about this. Every time I look at him, I see myself about to make the same damned fool mistake a second time and all I can think about is doing whatever I have to do to prevent it."

"If he's determined to make that mistake, there's really not much you can do about it, Colby. Like it or not, at nineteen, he's a man."

"There ought to be a law against nineteen-year-olds being men."

Diana laughed. "I can imagine how you would respond to that statement if you were nineteen again."

"You've made your point." He ran a hand through his damp hair. "What a mess." Colby got to his feet and walked restlessly to the front of the cavern. Hands on hips, he studied the situation.

"It's not getting any lighter out there, is it?" Diana called from the back of the cave.

"No." He turned around and returned to his place on the rocks. "It's worse than ever. Diana, if we don't get out of here by nightfall, we may have to spend the night in here. I don't want to take you down that ledge path after dark, even with flashlights."

"*What?*"

"Don't sound so horrified. It'll be a little cold and a little damp, not to mention a little uncomfortable, but we'll survive."

But Diana was genuinely horrified. The thought of spending the night in Chained Lady Cave shook her to the core. "We can't stay here, Colby. We don't have any food . . . or blankets, or matches."

"Don't worry about it until we have to make the decision."

"I'm worrying about it!" she yelped.

"Well, don't."

"Easy for you to say. Colby, I will not stay the night here and that's final."

"Honey, I'm trying to explain that you may not have a choice in the matter."

"I'll have a choice," she informed him grimly. "I've got a flashlight, and I'll find my way down that path alone if need be."

"The hell you will," he said far too quietly.

She slid him an uneasy, speculative glance.

"And turn off the flashlights. We may need them later. No sense wearing the batteries down now."

An hour later, night descended with no letup in the storm. If anything the gale was wilder than ever.

At least there was no fading sunlight to turn the waterfall into blood this evening, Diana told herself morosely. One had to be thankful for small mercies.

"Looks like the decision just got made for us," Colby said mildly. He reached out and switched on one of the flashlights. "We'll leave the other light off until this one burns out."

Diana jumped to her feet and hurried to the front of the cave. She was greeted by impenetrable blackness and a spray of water. Just beyond the entrance she could hear the relentless roar of the falls. Colby was right. No one in his or her right mind would attempt to negotiate the waterfall path tonight.

She sighed, resigned to a night in Chained Lady Cave, and turned to troop unhappily back to the damp rocks. She ran straight into Colby who had come up behind her. His arms went around her waist, and he bent his head to drop a reassuring kiss on her hair.

"It's going to be all right, honey."

"I'm cold already."

"We'll spread your slicker and my windbreaker out on the floor. They'll keep us reasonably dry. No fire, but never let it be said I don't know how to take care of my woman." He reached into his windbreaker pocket and produced two plastic packets of cheese and crackers.

Diana instantly felt better. "Where did you get those?"

"I just stuck them in at the last minute thinking we might want to have a snack up here before we hiked down."

"My hero!" she exclaimed admiringly. "I have a contribution to make to the effort, too." She reached into her trouser pocket, and pulled out a few sheets of facial tissue.

"What are we going to use that for? To wipe our hands after we eat?"

"Not exactly. It occurred to me it might come in useful for other reasons."

"You're planning on catching cold?"

"No, I am not planning on catching cold. Really, Colby. Use that vivid imagination of yours. Do you see any sanitary facilities around here?"

Understanding dawned. "Ah, I get it."

"Finally."

They ate the crackers and cheese snacks in less than three minutes.

"What we really need is a bottle of good wine to complement this fine cuisine," Colby remarked as he swallowed the last cracker crumb.

"At least neither of us has to cook tonight," Diana pointed out, trying to look on the positive side. "Specter will be okay, I think."

"Assuming he has sense enough to get in out of the rain."

"He knows where the back porch is. He can sleep there. Brandon and Robyn will be worried about us, though."

"They'll probably assume I got caught at your place in the storm and decided to spend the night." Colby paused and swore under his breath. "Which will leave them perfectly free to entertain themselves this evening, won't it?"

Diana read his mind. It wasn't hard to tell the direction of his thoughts. "Stop worrying about it," she advised gently. "If they're sleeping together, they're sleeping together. There's not much you can do about it."

"I know. I'll just have to keep my fingers crossed that Brandon was paying attention during all those lectures on birth control I gave him."

"Yup. Keeping your fingers crossed is about all you can do. Now stop fretting, and let's figure out where we're going to spread this rain gear." Diana jumped to her feet.

Colby looked at her, his eyes watchful in the faint glow of the flashlight beam. "I hate to point this out, but the fact is, it's dryer in the inner cavern. Also warmer. That's why I spent the night in there the last time."

"I don't like it in there," Diana said instantly. "I don't exactly love it out here, but I prefer this chamber to that grotto." She peered at the floor of the main cave, trying to find a spot that wasn't soaking wet. It was useless. "Maybe it will be more comfortable to sit up all night."

"I doubt it."

"Then *you* think of something, damn it!"

His brows rose. "You're really on edge, aren't you? Here, let me see that slicker of yours."

Wordlessly she handed it to him. A few minutes later he had it spread across a fairly smooth stretch of stone. He used his windbreaker to add some width to the sleeping surface, and then he sat down on top of the slicker and began removing his damp shoes. When he looked up to see what was keeping her from following suit, he smiled and held out his hand.

"Honey, this is as good as it's going to get tonight. Come on down here, and we'll try to get some sleep."

"I won't be able to sleep a wink tonight."

"Sure you will. Take off your shoes and get your feet dry. That will help."

She let him remove her sport shoes, and he was right. Things did seem more bearable when her feet were dry. When he was finished, he lay down, tangled her legs between his and cradled her, spoon-fashion.

"I don't think I'll ever go into a cave again as long as I live," Diana vowed.

"This wasn't my idea."

"Don't remind me." She turned and gave him a quick kiss. "I'm sorry for having gotten us into this mess."

"It's not so bad and it's not your fault. No one could have predicted that storm."

"It was a surprise, wasn't it?"

"Damn weird, if you want to know the truth."

"Don't say that. I'm nervous enough about this cave. Don't start implying the storm is some sort of supernatural event. I already know I'm not going to be able to sleep a wink."

Five minutes later, Diana was sound asleep.

Colby stirred beside her, trying to get comfortable. He stared into the blackness above, aware of how weak the flashlight beam was becoming. He wouldn't switch on the other one unless Diana awoke. As long as she was sleeping this soundly, she wouldn't miss the artificial illumination.

Never in all the years of growing up in Fulbrook Corners had he ever seen a storm as bad as the one that was blowing tonight. The wind seemed to have intensified in the past half hour. It was blowing with enough force now to send sprays of water off the falls straight into the main cavern. If it got any worse, he and Diana would both be soaked to the skin by morning.

Common sense told him they would both be dryer and far more comfortable in the back of the cave.

Colby sat up and looked down at Diana curled up beside him. Her tawny hair was tumbled around her shoulders and her lashes looked very long lying against her cheek. He was just beginning to realize how very important she had become to him lately. His obsession with her had not ended when he'd finally gotten her into bed. A part of him was starting to wonder if it would ever end.

Just what he needed, he thought wryly—an independent, assertive, opinionated career woman. A woman who'd never had children of her own but who felt qualified to lecture him on how to handle his own son.

But he wanted to know the rest of her secrets. He felt as if he'd only peeled away one thin layer of her complex personality. He needed to learn so much more about her.

First things first, however. His primary task tonight was to shield her from the storm. Another spray of water sailed in through the entrance.

Colby got to his feet and reached down to lift Diana into his arms. He picked up the flashlights and started toward the inner grotto.

Sometimes a man had to ride roughshod over a woman's fears for her own good. With any luck she wouldn't wake up until morning.

7

DIANA CAME PARTIALLY AWAKE, dimly aware of a dream that was fading rapidly. She couldn't remember any of the details, but she was awash in a gentle sea of wistful longing and deep, aching sensuality. She felt a little sad but did not understand why. She was also aware of a distant glimmer of hope, but she didn't understand that, either.

She waited for the dreamy state to subside, and when it didn't she shifted languidly, wondering why the bed seemed so hard tonight. Then she felt the weight of a man's leg lying across her thigh, and a vague recollection of the day's events surfaced.

She managed to get her eyes open just far enough to see the reassuring beam of the flashlight. It was definitely on its last legs, but she didn't have the energy to reach over and switch on the backup light.

"Colby?" she whispered sleepily.

"It's all right," he murmured drowsily, cradling her closer. "I'm right here." His palm stroked over her breast and he dropped a kiss onto her shoulder.

Diana closed her eyes again, feeling safe and secure in his embrace. The wistful longing within her intensified, melding with the sensual warmth that was spreading through her limbs. She turned toward Colby, instinctively trying to get closer. Her arm went around his lean waist.

"You feel good," she muttered. Her hand moved along his back, savoring the hard, contoured muscles. "Warm and strong."

"You feel good, too. Soft. Very soft. Sweet." He kissed her again, a sleepy caress on her brow and then the tip of her nose. She felt his body growing taut.

"Colby?" She slid her foot between his legs, and he instantly tightened his thighs, chaining her.

"Sweetheart," he breathed just before his mouth found hers.

Diana parted her lips for him, inviting him into her warmth and then there were no more words.

Colby's kiss grew suddenly fierce with a hunger that Diana responded to instantly. She welcomed the fierceness in him, knowing that it would never be used against her, knowing that with this man she was safe.

Passion flared without any warning, sweeping Diana into the heart of a swirling storm that seemed as intense as the one howling outside the cave. Colby's arms tightened around her. He rolled onto his back and pulled her with him. Then his hands locked in her hair.

She felt him lift himself against her, and her hands slid up under his shirt. She loved the feel of him. She couldn't get enough of it. Her whole body was beginning to sing with the joy only his lovemaking could give her.

She wanted to join with him, become one with him, love him.

When he unbuttoned her shirt and tossed it aside, she reacted in kind. His shirt landed on the cavern floor beside hers. He fumbled with her pants, his hands gliding warmly over her curving buttocks as he swept the last of her garments from her body.

She slid down along the length of him, and he began to breathe heavily as she stopped long enough to drop tiny kisses here and there across his broad chest.

When she unfastened and unzipped his jeans, Colby's hands tightened again in her hair. Wordlessly he lifted his hips against her, letting her know the full extent of his arousal. She reached into the opening of his jeans, cupping him intimately. And then her hair flowed over his thighs as she worshipped him with her mouth.

Colby groaned, enduring the sweet torture for as long as possible. But in the next moment he was lifting her and pushing her onto her back. He rose, looming over her for a long moment as he studied her nude body in the weak gleam of the flashlight. His hand moved along her thigh until he reached the flowing liquid warmth that marked her own desire.

Gently he stroked with his fingers until Diana thought she would fly apart into a thousand pieces. A moment later, when he touched her with his tongue, she knew she was lost.

The world spun around her. Her body was an exotic instrument that only Colby knew how to play. She clutched at him, writhed against him, sobbed out her feminine demands.

And finally he came to her, burying himself deep within her until she was filled with him and he was surrounded by her. The white-hot heat of their mutual passion exploded around them, enveloping them. They clung together, whirling about in an endless universe that knew no beginning and no end.

Diana gave herself completely, bestowing herself as only a woman in love can when she knows she has found the right mate. It was a total capitulation to her own passion and to her lover's. It was the kind of surrender that forever chains the conqueror.

This time it was right. This time they were meant to be together. This time she was free to give that which he could never take from her by force. And she gave it to him willingly, with all her heart, knowing the time had come at last.

Past, present and future were now linked.

Diana cried out, and Colby drank the sound from her lips.

When it was over, neither spoke. They fell into an exhausted sleep in each others' arms.

HE DRESSED SLOWLY, watching her come awake in the glow of the remaining flashlight. He wondered what she would say about the violent passion that had taken them both by storm in the middle of the night.

Would she be angry at his carelessness? Or would she retreat into that self-contained, fiercely independent part of herself and act as if nothing had happened?

It hadn't been a dream, he was honest enough with himself to admit that, but there had been an odd, dreamlike quality to the whole thing. Should he say something first?

No, he decided. Let her bring up the subject if she wants to. Let her decide to say something about it, if something needs to be said. What had happened had been an unplanned accident. Neither of them was to blame. Both of them were responsible.

Colby knew he was searching for excuses, and there were none. Neither of them had any excuse except the age-old one of ungovernable passion. That passion had descended swiftly, taking them by surprise while they were both half-drugged with sleep. It had swept them both into a shattering conflagration of the senses and then cast them adrift, allowing them to lose themselves once more in sleep.

The passion had dominated him so completely that he hadn't remembered to use the contents of the little foil packet in his wallet. And she hadn't thought about it, either.

All of which added up to the fact that Diana might even now be pregnant.

Colby wondered why he wasn't more alarmed at the thought. By rights, he should be chewing his fingernails to the quick this morning. He hadn't had this kind of reason to worry since he'd been nineteen.

She would be upset, he knew. A little scared, perhaps. Even at her age she was bound to be nervous about this. Maybe he should say something first.

But what could he say? Sorry, I forgot? I woke up in the middle of the night in a cave and you were in my arms and I had to have you, and nothing in this world could have stopped me from taking you?

Because that's the way it had been for him. At his age, that excuse wasn't worth the breath it took to say it.

Diana stirred and opened her eyes. She focused on the dull glow of the flashlight for a moment, obviously trying to get her bearings.

"Colby?"

"Right here, honey." He leaned over and kissed her bare shoulder. "You as stiff and sore as I am?"

"I may not be able to sit up, let alone walk again."

He smiled, telling himself he was relieved that she wasn't going to start out the morning by berating him, even though he deserved it. But part of him was irritated by her calm attitude. Was she going to ignore the whole thing? Diana could be so strong-minded. A regular amazon.

He eased himself to a sitting position and helped her to sit up beside him. Then he began massaging her shoulders with an easy familiarity. She sighed and leaned into the brisk rubdown.

"Better?" he asked. She looked good in the morning, he thought—even after having spent the night on a stone floor—sweet, vulnerable, relaxed and sexy.

"Much better. Colby, we're in the grotto room. How on earth did we get in here? I don't remember moving." She stared around with a small frown. Then she seemed to notice the clothes that were scattered around them.

Maybe she didn't remember any of it, he thought, jolted. After all, she had been half-asleep. "I carried you in here when the wind started whipping the water into the main chamber. We'd have been drenched by now if we'd stayed out there."

"Oh. Thanks, I guess. But the sooner we get out of here, the better. No offense, but there's something about this place that really gives me the creeps."

"Were you scared last night?" Colby asked quietly as he got to his feet.

She looked at him in surprise. "No, not really. I don't like the place, but I have to admit I didn't suffer any real claustrophobia in here. I slept amazingly well, in fact, all things considered." She got to her feet, dressing quickly. "How about you? Scared to your toes like last time?"

He shook his head. Why wasn't she saying anything about the unplanned and unprotected lovemaking? She was acting as if nothing out of the ordinary had happened even as she put on the clothes that he'd removed last night in the heat of passion. "No. It wasn't the same as last time at all." Nothing had ever felt so right, in fact, as making love to Diana on the floor of the grotto. He was chagrined that she wasn't going to mention it. He felt like asking, *Was it good for you, too?* just to see what she would say.

"Hope that storm has stopped," Diana was saying in a conversational tone.

"Come on, let's see what's going on out there. You ready to go?"

"Believe me, I have no desire to hang around here." She made to follow him out of the little grotto. "I will say, however, that this is probably the most unusual date I've ever been on in my life."

"As a writer of horror fiction I felt I had a reputation to live up to. A guy like me can't take his lady on plain, ordinary dates. She might begin to think he was a fraud."

"You've got a point."

She was going to handle this with her usual self-contained manner, he realized. So be it. If she didn't want to talk about it, damned if he was going to say anything. But he realized he was now thoroughly irritated. The woman was too independent for her own good. She took on too much responsibility—accepted all the risks. Hell, he was a part of what had happened. She should be talking to him about it, not dealing with it all on her own.

He wondered for the first time if Diana had ever in her life turned to a man in a time of crisis—ever leaned on a male when the going got tough—ever asked one to share responsibility with her.

The more he got to know her, the more he doubted it. He wondered what it would take to get her to turn to him for help and comfort. Probably a full-scale natural disaster—say, an earthquake that registered around eight or nine on the scale.

Colby stepped out into the main cavern and relaxed as he saw the veil of white water roaring past the cave entrance. "We're in luck. Sun's out and the wind has stopped. Shouldn't be any trouble getting down that path now."

"I hope we haven't caused Brandon and Robyn any worry."

"I just hope they haven't caused me any more worry," Colby retorted. "I've got enough problems at the moment."

Diana gave him an odd glance but said nothing as he led her down the ledge path.

COLBY DROPPED DIANA OFF at her cottage, exchanged a few epithets with a disgruntled Specter, who had taken offense at having been left alone all night, and drove back to Aunt Jesse's place. A glance at his watch showed it was only seven o'clock. Brandon was an early riser like his father, but Colby had a hunch Robyn wouldn't have gotten out of bed yet. That suited Colby just fine. It would give him an opportunity to talk calmly to Brandon.

Maybe Diana had a point, he thought as he parked the Jeep and took the porch steps two at a time. Maybe the kid was trapped and had come looking for a way out. At nineteen, it was too damned easy for a man to get himself between the devil and the deep blue sea.

Especially when a woman was involved.

He'd back off, Colby decided resolutely. He'd try Diana's advice. He'd give Brandon a chance to come to him—an opportunity to talk without feeling threatened. He and Brandon had always had a good relationship. Now was the time to fall back on nineteen years of a solid father-son bond.

He walked into the house and heard the door of Robyn's room closing upstairs. A few seconds later, Brandon came ambling down the stairs toward the kitchen, yawning. He was wearing a T-shirt and a pair of jeans. He was barefoot and still busy fastening the snap of his denims.

All Colby's good resolutions went out the window.

"If you haven't got brains enough to keep your pants zipped around her, I hope you've at least got enough brains to be taking precautions."

Brandon halted halfway down the stairs, startled. "*Dad...* I didn't hear the Jeep. When did you get back? Where were you last night? We wondered what had happened."

"Doesn't look like you spent too much time worrying about my whereabouts." Colby slammed into the kitchen and filled Aunt Jesse's old dented kettle. He set it on the stove and started to shovel instant coffee into a large mug. He was aware of Brandon standing uneasily in the doorway.

"I sort of figured you were at Diana's," Brandon muttered.

Colby tried to get control of his frustrated anger. "I was with her. We got caught in the cave behind Chained Lady Falls. Had to spend the night there." He swung around. "Damn it, Brandon, have you got any idea of the risks you're taking?"

"I'm probably not taking any more risks than you and Diana are taking," Brandon shot back.

Colby winced as memories of the night swamped him. "Are you using something?" he asked roughly. "Or are you relying on Robyn?"

Brandon flushed. "Geez, Dad . . ."

"Just answer me, okay?"

"I've got protection. Don't worry, we're not taking any chances. For crying out loud, after all those books you had me read, and after all those talks you gave me on the subject, how could I forget to use something?"

"Sometimes it's too damn easy to forget. Believe me, I know." The kettle began to shriek. Colby swiped it off the stove and poured boiling water into the mug. Too damn easy.

"You're so afraid I'm going to make the same mistake you made—you can't get past that, can you?" Brandon asked moodily. He trooped over to the table and flung himself down in a chair.

"Yeah, that's exactly what scares me."

"What's so bad about getting married at my age?" Brandon asked.

Colby started to lose his temper all over again. Then it occurred to him that if Diana's theory was right, his son's question might be a legitimate opening for rational discussion, not a challenge. With great effort, he got control of his anger. "You want some coffee?"

Brandon gave him a surprised glance. "Sure."

Colby fixed another mug of instant and carried it over to the table. He sat down across from Brandon and stared out at the bright, sunny morning for a moment. "You really want to know what's so bad about getting married at your age?"

Brandon toyed with his mug, giving the impression he was already regretting the question. "I know it might be a little rough trying to finish school while being married, but . . ."

"Rough?" Colby leaned forward, his elbows on the table. "You want to know what rough is? I'll tell you. Rough is wondering how you're going to pay the rent when you've just lost your job and you can't get another because you don't have any experience or fancy degrees. Rough is having to worry about a young wife who gets bored and restless after the novelty of being married wears off and she has to sit home while her girlfriends are out on dates."

"Dad . . ."

"Rough is wishing you could be going windsurfing with the other guys instead of having to hunt for another job and entertain a wife who by now wishes she'd never married you because marriage isn't nearly as much fun as she had thought it would be. Rough is worrying about diaper rash, fevers in the middle of the night, crying that sometimes goes on and on until you think you're going to go out of your mind."

"But, Dad . . ."

"But do you know what the roughest thing of all is? It's realizing that you married before you really understood what you needed from a woman. It's realizing that sex isn't everything, even though, at nineteen, it seems like the most important thing in the world. It's realizing you made a mistake and that there's no going back."

Brandon looked at him. "Is that the way it was for you?"

Colby took a swallow of coffee. "Yeah, that's the way it was for me."

"And you think that's the way it's going to be for me?"

"I think that's the way it would be for anyone who gets married too young."

There was silence for a moment. "Robyn thinks it will work out."

"Does she? How does she know?"

"I don't know." Brandon hunched over his coffee. "She really wants to get married."

"Do you?" Colby asked bluntly.

Brandon's shoulders moved restlessly. "Sometimes I think it would be all right, you know? I really like her, Dad."

"That's obvious. But do you really like the idea of marriage?"

"Last night I told her maybe we should wait a while." The words came slowly, stiffly. "I said maybe next summer we could talk about it again."

This was probably as much as he could hope for right now, Colby told himself. He could hear Diana telling him not to blow it now. The kid had come more than halfway. "Sounds reasonable," he said cautiously.

"She didn't think so. She doesn't like the idea of waiting. She's got it hard at home, you know?"

Something in Brandon's tone told Colby that Robyn had been more than a little upset. Was that how Brandon had ended up in the girl's bed? Had Robyn tried to give him a graphic demonstration of the wonders of married life?

"It's your life too, Brandon. You don't have to live it the way she wants you to live it. You have a responsibility to do what you think is best, not what anyone else tells you is best. All I ask is that you make your own decision while you've still got all your options open."

"I'm thinking about it," Brandon said stubbornly. "You've got to understand Robyn's parents, though. They try to run her life. Always yelling at her. Always fighting."

"Tell me something, son. If you were having the kind of trouble at home that Robyn is having, would you look for someone else to rescue you or would you rescue yourself?"

Brandon scowled. "I'd get myself out of the house. But that's different."

"Is it? If you did use someone else to rescue you, do you think you would ever really feel free?"

"No, not exactly."

"Do you want to deny Robyn the experience of learning how to get herself free? Do you want her to exchange her dominating parents for a husband she thinks will replace them? She'll expect you to step right into the role of taking care of her. But she figures you won't treat her the way they do. You won't yell at her. I'll tell you something, Brandon. After a few months of taking care of her, you probably would be yelling at her. You'd realize she married you only because she wanted to use you."

Brandon looked up, a faint bewilderment in his fine brown eyes. "Sometimes it's hard to think straight about things like that, isn't it? I mean, when you're with a girl and she starts talking about marriage and stuff while you're thinking about other things, and you want her to be happy but you also want to go to bed with her, and she knows that and sort of uses that to . . . oh hell. You know what I mean."

For the first time since Brandon had arrived, Colby took genuine pity on his son. He gave him a slow, man-to-man grin. "Brandon, good buddy, allow me to tell you that I know exactly what you mean. Welcome to the club. You're learning the hard way what every man apparently learns the hard way. At the age of forty, I have come to the conclusion there is no easy way to learn it. Women can complicate a man's life no end."

"Does Diana complicate your life?"

Colby drummed his fingers on the tabletop. "Enormously. And the worst of it is, I don't think she even realizes it."

DIANA DROVE INTO TOWN later that morning with Specter sitting beside her.

"The trouble with men," she informed the dog, "is that they can really complicate a woman's life. They're so damned difficult to understand. They don't think logically or rationally, the way a woman does. They don't know how to analyze their emotions or themselves. They don't communicate well. They just sort of blunder into your life and stumble around trying to get your attention. When they have it, they don't know what to do with it."

Specter whined in sympathy and then stuck his nose out the window to sample the morning smells.

"He never said a word this morning, the bastard. Not one word. I would have sworn he didn't even remember making love to me, except that he obviously had to get dressed, the same as I did. He must have realized why he'd taken off his clothes in the first place. Specter, we went crazy last night. We just woke up and went crazy. I've never taken that kind of risk before. What if something happens? I think I'm getting scared."

Specter pulled his large muzzle back out of the slipstream and gave her a curious glance. Diana sighed and reached out to pat him reassuringly. "If I'm pregnant, I'll let you have Colby, okay? I know you've been looking for an excuse to sink your teeth into his throat."

Specter yipped at the name.

"All we can do is wait and see," Diana said gloomily. "The odds are in my favor, I think, although it couldn't have happened at a worse time of the month. But it was only one night and after all, I am thirty-four. I've heard it's more difficult to get pregnant in your thirties than it is when you're younger." She groaned. "But I have to tell you truthfully, Specter. The man felt very fertile to me last night."

She was still trying to comprehend her own incomprehensible behavior. Her romantic relationships had been few and far between and always conducted with great caution and discretion. She had never in her life awakened in the middle of the night and surrendered to overwhelming passion the way she had last night. She still couldn't believe it had been her in that cave.

There was no sign of Colby's Jeep in the post office lot, but Margaret Fulbrook's aging Cadillac was parked there when Diana arrived. The woman was not in the car, but her unsmiling, heavyset, odd-job man was sitting in the front seat.

"Just my luck," Diana told Specter as she opened the car door and got out. "Maybe she'll ignore me." She didn't really feel like dealing with Margaret Fulbrook today. The woman's bitterness was enough to chill the soul of anyone who got too close to her.

But Margaret Fulbrook didn't ignore Diana. She came through the glass doors just as Diana was about to open them. Diana held the door for her, reflecting philosophically on the ingrained nature of one's personal manners.

"You're that woman Savagar has taken up with for the summer, aren't you?" Margaret Fulbrook demanded without any preamble. Her dark eyes glittered in her rigidly set face.

"I'm Diana Prentice," Diana said mildly.

"I want to talk to you."

Diana's eyes widened. "You do?"

"Come with me." She brushed past Diana, heading toward the Cadillac. The woman was obviously accustomed to giving orders and having them obeyed.

Diana shrugged and followed warily. She watched as the grim-faced Harry climbed ponderously out of the Cadillac and opened the passenger door for his employer.

"Thank you, Harry." Mrs. Fulbrook settled herself in the seat as if she were assuming her throne. She waited while Harry went back to the driver's side, and then she angled her fierce gaze up through the window. "Have you seen my grandson?"

She should have been expecting that question, Diana realized. But she'd been preoccupied with other things this morning. "I've met him, yes. I had dinner with him and Colby the other night."

"I'm told he has the Fulbrook eyes. Is that true?"

Diana gazed down at Margaret Fulbrook's intelligent brown eyes. "Yes, ma'am. He does. He's a very fine-looking young man."

"Heard he's got a girl with him. Probably takes after his father in that respect."

"He has a girlfriend, yes. Most young men do at that age." Diana braced one palm against the roof of the Cadillac and said casually, "He's just finished his first year in college. Doing very well, I gather. I believe he plans on becoming an engineer."

Margaret Fulbrook snorted. "Maybe he'll amount to more than his father ever did."

Diana couldn't repress a smile. "If you're talking about financial success, Mrs. Fulbrook, I assure you, Colby's done just fine."

"I read one of those terrible books of his. Complete nonsense. Nothing but monsters and blood and gore. The stuff of nightmares."

"Not everybody can write a nightmare. Colby has a real talent."

"That bastard. He hasn't got any talent. Leastways, not any respectable talent." But there was little heat in the words. It was as if Mrs. Fulbrook had called Colby a bastard so many times during the past twenty years that she could no longer summon up much venom.

"I imagine his publisher would disagree with you," Diana said gently.

"Bah. What do I care about his publisher?" The woman was silent for a long moment, staring straight ahead through the windshield. "What's he like?" she asked at last.

"Who, Colby?"

"No! Not Savagar." White lines appeared on either side of the woman's mouth. "I know well enough what he's like. He's a seducer of innocent young girls. He's a shiftless, no-account, sleazy opportunist who tried to take the easy way out by marrying my daughter. But it all backfired on him. I made sure he never got a dime. Not one thin dime, by God."

"Did he ever ask for a dime?"

"That's beside the point! If he never asked, it's because he figured out fast enough I'd never give him anything. I am not interested in Colby Savagar. I was asking you what my grandson is like. Did Savagar ruin him completely?"

"Brandon is an intelligent, well-educated, well-mannered, well-spoken, surprisingly sensitive young man. I like him very much."

"No doubt you've been brainwashed by Savagar."

"No doubt."

"Nineteen years," Margaret Fulbrook said slowly. "Nineteen years. And I haven't seen Cynthia's son since the funeral."

"Who's fault is that?"

"Savagar's, of course. He never brought the boy to see me."

"I imagine that's because he knew you wanted nothing to do with himself or Brandon. I gather you made your wishes clear at the funeral."

"I still don't want anything to do with Colby Savagar. But when I heard the boy was in town, I... wondered."

Diana drew a deep breath and took the plunge. "Brandon asked me about you yesterday."

The silvered head snapped around. "He did?"

"I think he's curious about you. He has no kin except for his father. It's perfectly natural that since he's here in Fulbrook Corners, he might start wondering about his mother's people."

"Probably wonders how much money he can get out of me. The boy was raised by his father and he'll have turned out just like him."

Diana hid another smile. "I'll admit that Brandon is a lot like his father. But he definitely has his mother's eyes. Goodbye, Mrs. Fulbrook. I'm sure you're busy and I've got to go pick up my mail. See you around." She stepped back from the car.

"One moment, young woman!"

It was nice to be called a young woman, Diana reflected in amusement as she turned back. "Yes, Mrs. Fulbrook?"

"If you had a lick of sense or an ounce of decency and self-respect, you'd stop seeing Savagar. He'll do you no good, and the bastard doesn't deserve to be happy, even for the short time he'll keep you around."

Diana looked down at her, astonished. "I beg your pardon?"

"You heard me." There was a relentless malice in the glittering brown gaze. "I saw the way Savagar looked at you the other day in the post office. He's finding happiness with you, and he has no right to that. He has no right to happiness of any kind. He deserves to be punished for what he did to my daughter. Stop seeing him!"

Margaret Fulbrook rolled up the window to cut off further conversation, and a few seconds later the heavy car lumbered out of the parking lot. Diana stood and watched until it was out of sight.

8

WHEN DIANA WALKED BACK into the cottage half an hour later, her arms full of groceries and Specter at her heels, she almost didn't notice the flowers in the vase on the hall table.

The bright yellow and white daisies were gone. In their place was a bunch of colorless, decaying weeds.

Diana nearly dropped her packages. "Specter," she whispered.

Instantly he was there, pushing a concerned, inquiring nose against her thigh. Then he pressed forward, sniffing around the base of the hall table. He gave a sharp bark and looked at her.

"Somebody's been in here." Diana glanced around nervously. She knew there was no one else in the house at the moment. Specter would have gone crazy. Slowly, she went on into the kitchen, half-afraid of what she might find.

But there was nothing out of place, nothing missing. She let the grocery sacks slide out of her arms onto the tiled countertop and then made herself walk deliberately from room to room. Specter hovered close, sensing her uneasiness. But he obviously knew there was no immediate threat.

Diana went back out into the hall and stared at the unsightly clump of weeds.

"It's a joke," she told Specter, trying to reassure herself. "Someone's playing a very strange joke." But there was something unsettlingly familiar about this particular prank. It took Diana a minute to remember, and then her memory clicked. "There was an incident like this in Colby's book."

Whirling around, she hurried into the kitchen and picked up *Shock Value*. Her fingers trembled slightly as she turned the pages, searching for the right scene. "So help me, Specter, if this is his idea of comedy, I'll wring his neck. This is not funny."

She found the scene in the third chapter. Donnelly had just walked into his home and discovered that a beautiful arrangement of gladioli had been replaced with a ragged assortment of dead weeds.

Shock sliced through him slowly, a dull blade inching along the nerve endings of his spine. He stared at the moldering weeds, knowing they were both an offering and a warning. Their stench filled the air. They trailed limply out of the crystal vase, evil doppelgängers of the fresh, lush blooms they had replaced.

An offering and a warning.

They were tribute to the dark being which the local people believed haunted the cove, and they were also meant as a warning to Donnelly who refused to take such legends seriously.

A passionate rage seized him. He reached out and jerked the weeds from the beautiful vase. He tossed the dead things onto the hearth and watched with satisfaction as the fire eagerly consumed them.

It wasn't until the weeds had been reduced to ashes that Donnelly asked himself who could have placed them in the vase. He didn't like any of the possible answers.

Diana slowly closed the door. "I don't like any of the answers, either, Specter."

The sound of Colby's Jeep in her drive brought her out of the kitchen and sent Specter bounding to the front door. The dog growled his usual warning as Colby came up the steps.

"Diana?" Colby let himself into the cottage. The screen door slammed behind him. "Out of my way, Specter. I've got better things to do than trade insults with you today. Some other time, maybe. *Diana?*"

"I'm right here, Colby," she said quietly. She stood in the kitchen doorway and watched him walk heedlessly past the weeds.

His brows rose. "Something wrong?"

Her eyes went to the table beside him. Automatically he followed her gaze. At first he looked puzzled, and then his eyes narrowed.

"I found them there when I got home a few minutes ago. When I left this morning, there were daisies in that vase. Remind you of anything, Colby?"

"Damn." He looked back at her. "Yeah, it reminds me of something. A scene out of one of my books."

"*Shock Value.*"

"Got that far, did you?" He snatched the weeds out of the vase and strode into the kitchen where he tossed them into the garbage. "So who the hell put them in your vase and why?"

Diana folded her arms, unconsciously withdrawing into herself. She was glad to have the weeds gone but the ramifications of the situation could not be dismissed so easily. "I don't know. I thought you might have some ideas."

"Me?" His expression darkened further. "What is this? You thought I might have done it?"

"It occurred to me that maybe this was some sort of joke to tease me about how long it's taking me to read *Shock Value*."

Colby swore again, this time more crudely. Specter muttered a warning and edged closer to his mistress. Colby ignored the dog. He opened the refrigerator door and helped himself to a can of beer he had stored in there a few days earlier.

"Just so you'll know in the future," he said roughly as he opened the beer, "I am not into practical jokes."

Diana drew a breath of relief. "I'm sorry," she whispered. "It's just that for a few minutes I was very frightened, and I guess it was easier to think it might have been you staging a stupid prank than to think that some stranger was in here today."

Colby watched her face for a moment and then his eyes softened. "Come here, honey," he said gently and held out his hand.

Diana hesitated, and then with a small, wordless exclamation, she stepped close and let him fold her against his side. She leaned into him, allowing herself to take comfort and reassurance from his strength. He held her with one arm wrapped securely around her and sipped his beer thoughtfully.

"When I figure out who put the weeds in your vase, I'll beat him to a pulp," Colby finally announced.

Specter gave a small yip. Colby looked down at the dog. "Okay, pal, you can help me."

"Who would do such a thing, Colby?"

"Damned if I know, but we've got a town full of possible candidates."

"What do you mean by that?" Diana demanded.

"In case it has escaped your notice, sweetheart, I am not exactly the favorite son of Fulbrook Corners. I've got a lot of old enemies."

"After twenty years? I doubt that."

"Some folks around here have long memories, believe me. And not everyone is glad I didn't wind up in jail. The general consensus in Fulbrook Corners was that sooner or later I'd come to a bad end. People don't like to be proven wrong."

She heard the old anger in his voice and slipped an arm around his lean waist. "Colby, even if you're right, you're overlooking something. The prank was played on me, not you."

"I hate to break this to you, Diana, but you're a logical target."

"Why?"

"Because everyone in town knows you belong to me."

"Don't be ridiculous!" Indignantly, Diana started to pull away from him. His arms tightened, drawing her firmly back against his side. "I don't belong to anyone."

But Colby wasn't paying any attention to her protest. His brows were knit together in a frown of concentration. "It would be easy enough for almost any of these turkeys around here to figure out that the surest method of getting back at me would be through you."

"Colby, that is an illogical assumption, but even if we go ahead and assume it for the sake of argument, we're still stuck with the question of who would do such a thing."

"Well, for starters, we know it's someone who read *Shock Value*."

"Hah. From what I understand, that includes just about everybody around here. Why, even this morning Margaret Fulbrook told me she'd read one of your books. . . ." Diana floundered to a halt as Colby pinned her with a sharp glare.

"You talked to Margaret Fulbrook today?"

"She was just coming out of the post office as I was going in. We exchanged a few words."

"About the weather?"

"No, damn it, not about the weather." Diana sighed. "She wanted to know if I'd met her grandson."

"What did you tell her?"

"The truth, of course. I told her Brandon was a very charming, intelligent young man." Diana paused and then added tentatively, "I think she'd like to meet him, Colby."

"I'll see her in hell before I let her near Brandon."

"Oh, Colby, be reasonable. She's an old woman and she doesn't have much left."

"That's her problem. Don't waste your pity on her, Diana. She doesn't deserve it." Colby swallowed more beer. "But I suppose we could start our list of possible pranksters with her. God knows she thinks she's got reason enough to hate me. And she knows about you."

Diana winced, remembering the woman's warning to her earlier. *Stay away from Colby Savagar. He has no right to happiness of any kind.* No point mentioning that bit of vindictiveness to Colby. He'd pounce on it as evidence of Margaret Fulbrook's guilt. Diana went for logic.

"She's an old woman, Colby. Whoever did this had to rush out here while I was in town."

"She's got Harry to run her around. Harry always felt honored to run errands for the Fulbrooks. Old man Fulbrook sent him after me when Cynthia said she was pregnant. Harry was real happy with the job."

Diana's eyes widened. "Fulbrook sent Harry after you? Why?"

"Why do you think? To beat some sense into me. Get me to leave town. Harry was twenty years younger then and built like an ox. And he never did like me in the first place."

"What happened?"

"He caught up with me outside the old Rawlins place. I'd been out talking to Eddy Spooner, and I was on my way back to Aunt Jesse's. Harry blocked the road with one of the Fulbrook trucks and when I stopped, he got out and pulled me out of my car. Said he was going to give me what I had coming to me. Then he started swinging a length of pipe at my head."

"My God, Colby."

"Fortunately he missed on the first swing, and I didn't give him a chance to get lucky with the second one. He was big, but he wasn't very fast on his feet. The trick to handling guys like Harry the Ox is to have a sucker punch up your sleeve. I managed to kick him where it would do the most good. He went down yelling. I jumped in the car and got out of there. Nobody could catch me in a car in those days." Colby paused reflectively. "Sucker wrecked my windshield with that first swing of the pipe, though. I never collected from him for the damage."

Diana was shaken. "Maybe we have to add Harry to the list."

"Uh-huh. I'm afraid he's one of many."

"Colby, for pete's sake, what did you do as a kid? Run around getting into fights with everyone in town?"

He flashed her an outrageous grin. "From my point of view, it was the other way around. Everyone was always trying to pick a fight with me."

"And you obliged."

He shrugged. "Sure. Why not?"

Diana lightly punched his shoulder. "You big macho idiot. You enjoyed your reputation, didn't you? You liked being a local legend. No wonder you've got a list of non-friends a mile long. How are we ever going to figure out who put those weeds in my vase?"

"Violence will accomplish nothing. At least, not violence against me." Colby made a production out of rubbing his wounded shoulder. Then his eyes grew thoughtful once more. "That's a hell of a good question. Gossip travels fast in a town like this. Eddy Spooner may have heard something down at the gas station. I'll talk to him. In the meantime, whenever I'm not around, make sure you keep that stupid hound of yours close. He should be capable of defending you against the kind of creep who plays practical jokes."

Specter wrinkled his nose.

"I think you've offended him," Diana said.

"Not a chance. Dog's not smart enough to figure out when he's been insulted. Now, about dinner tonight."

"What about it?"

"I was hoping you'd help me baby-sit. To tell you the truth, things are a little tense over at my place. Dear little Robyn is not happy with me."

"Why not?"

"Probably because she knows what you already figured out. My son isn't all that enthusiastic about marriage. I think you're right, Diana. I think he's gotten himself into a tangle, and he's looking for a polite way out. We had a long talk this morning."

Diana frowned. "If Robyn thinks she's losing Brandon, she's bound to be upset."

"Tell me about it. The kid looks at me as if I were an ogre. She's stopped telling me how fabulous my books are, too."

Diana grinned. "Ah, the fickle public."

"You'll come over for dinner?"

"Why don't the three of you come over here? Maybe a change of scene will relieve the tension. You think Robyn and Brandon will like stir-fry?"

"That's not the problem. Have you ever cooked for teenagers?"

"Well, no. What's the big secret?"

"The big secret is that you have to start by quadrupling the quantities of everything you fix."

"I was going to quadruple everything. After all, there will be four of us. I can count, Colby."

"No," Colby said patiently. "You don't understand. You quadruple the amounts for each teenager."

"Oh. I see. That's a lot of vegetables."

IT DIDN'T TAKE LONG to determine that Colby had been right about the tension between Brandon, Robyn and himself. Halfway through dinner, Diana felt she could cut the atmosphere with a knife. Robyn looked wounded and sullen. Brandon tried to respond to Diana's conversational gambits, but invariably he ran out of things to say.

It was Colby who finally generated some real conversation when he casually told Brandon and Robyn about the weeds in Diana's vase.

"Right out of *Shock Value*," Brandon said. "Who would do something like that? And why?"

"We're not sure," Colby said calmly. "I talked to Eddy Spooner this afternoon, but he hadn't heard any rumors or gossip. I told him to keep his eyes open, though."

"It's spooky," Robyn said slowly. She looked at Diana. "Were you scared?"

"It was very unnerving," Diana admitted. "Rather like getting an obscene phone call. I recognized the scene out of Colby's book, too, and it upset me."

"No need to worry as long as you've got good old Specter," Brandon said with a smile as he slipped a bite of stir-fried carrot under the table.

Colby scowled. "Are you feeding that dog under the table again? He doesn't deserve any treats. He's spoiled rotten as it is."

Diana smiled. "Maybe Specter would think more highly of you, Colby, if you slipped him a bite now and then."

"Over my dead body."

A low, enthusiastic growl rumbled from beneath the table. Diana looked at Brandon and they both laughed. Robyn pushed her food around on her plate, and Colby muttered something about the likelihood of a dog such as Specter biting the hand that fed it.

"How's the job hunting going?" Brandon asked equably.

"Not as well as it should," Diana responded. "I've got to get going on it if I want to find a good job by September. I really don't want to have to go back to Carruthers and Yale."

"Have you ever been married, Diana?" Robyn asked suddenly, her pretty blue eyes reflecting a touch of malice.

Colby glared at Robyn, but Diana answered patiently. "No, Robyn, I haven't."

"And you've never had any kids, either?"

"No."

"Why not?"

"Geez, Robyn," Brandon muttered. "It's not exactly your business, is it?"

"I just want to know what makes her such an expert on marriage."

Diana was startled. "Who said I was?"

"Brandon was telling me all about how women are putting off marriage these days so that they can get a good start on their careers," Robyn explained a little too sweetly. "He was using you as an example. I said you weren't a very good example because you probably never would marry or have kids. All you're interested in is your career."

"That's enough," Colby said coldly.

Diana felt a funny twinge in the pit of her stomach. For some reason she felt obliged to defend herself. "You can't always have it all, Robyn. I made some choices early on, and I haven't regretted them."

"You chose a career over marriage. I don't think that makes you a very good example for someone like me who wants something different out of life."

Colby leaned forward menacingly. "I said, that's enough, Robyn."

Diana forced a reassuring smile. "It's all right. I know what she means. But I'll defend to the hilt the importance of a young woman getting her education and establishing a career before she marries and has children."

"Lots of women get married before they worry about a career," Robyn insisted.

"No female in her right mind should ever put herself in a position of total economic dependence on a man. She should always be able to take care of herself financially. And if she plans to have children, it's even more important that she be capable of supporting an entire family by herself. Women too often wind up raising children alone these days, in case you haven't noticed."

"That wouldn't happen to me."

"I'm sure every woman who gets pregnant feels that way. But do you know who's filling up the ranks at the poverty line in this country? Single women and their children, that's who. The men who promised to take care of them are long gone."

Diana took a deep breath and realized Brandon was looking at her with something close to admiration. Robyn was obviously furious.

But it was Colby's expression that surprised Diana. He was scowling darkly.

DIANA CAME AWAKE with a shiver of dread. The dream hadn't been truly a nightmare, but it had been emotionally wrenching, nonetheless. She realized with a start that she was crying.

Specter woofed questioningly. He got to his feet and pushed his muzzle into her hand. Instinctively Diana stroked him, drawing some comfort from the process.

"I'm okay," she told the dog. "It was just a dream."

A dream of a terrible darkness. A horrifying aloneness. Uncounted eons of aloneness. And the feeling of a knife in her hand. Blood welling up under her fingers, trickling out of the cave to mingle with the water and the mist. A man's voice was speaking to her, his dying curse filling the grotto even as he rolled free of her body.

You have fought me to the death. I would not have believed a woman could be so stubborn, nor so valiant. If you had been born male, you would have been a mighty warrior.

But you have not won, woman. I die here now, but so will you. And by all the gods, I tell you this, you wretched female: I curse you. With my dying blood I curse you now. Listen well to your fate, for you cannot escape. Your spirit will remain chained here until you give me the child I seek. You will learn at last what it is to be a woman. The final victory will be mine. Yours, the ultimate surrender.

"I should never have let Colby tell me about the legend of Chained Lady Cave, Specter." Diana tossed back the covers and reached for her robe and slippers. "That man is too good at inducing nightmares."

She padded down the hall, too uneasy to go immediately back to sleep. Specter followed, always willing to indulge in a midnight snack.

"That dream was all I needed on top of finding those dead weeds in my vase today," Diana confided as she rummaged around in the refrigerator. She hadn't been this shaken by a dream in a long while. "What with dreams and weeds and worrying about being pregnant, I'll be lucky to get back to sleep tonight."

The cottage seemed chilled and far too quiet to her disturbed senses. She was very glad Specter was there in the kitchen with her. Diana was used to being alone but there were times when it would be nice to have a man around.

IT WAS THE DREAM AGAIN. More intense than ever. Probably because he'd spent the other night in Chained Lady Cave. Was he going to have this dream off and on for the rest of his life?

He stood at the downstairs window listening to the stillness of the house, and his mind drifted back to all the long nights he had spent here as a child. They were usually nights spent imagining the worst things that could happen to him.

Outside in the darkness, deep shadows pooled among the trees. Colby watched them for a while. Why had he come back here to this town? Why couldn't he shake the feeling that there was something here in Fulbrook Corners that remained unfinished? Maybe he was just realizing the simple psychological fact that the past was always part of the future.

Colby sighed. It was more than that. He had been drawn back here by a vague feeling of incompleteness. There was something here that needed to be done before he could really be free of Fulbrook Corners.

He swore under his breath. He wanted to see Diana. He needed her tonight. The cave dream was getting to him.

Colby turned away from the window, scrawled a brief note on a piece of paper and dropped the paper on the kitchen table. He'd probably be home before dawn.

Then again, he might not.

He decided to walk to Diana's. If he took the Jeep, he'd probably waken Brandon and Robyn.

Ten minutes later, he saw the light glowing from Diana's kitchen window and wondered at it. He quickened his pace and was on the first porch step when Specter's sharp bark sounded from within.

"It's me, Diana," he called reassuringly as he pounded on the door. "Call off your damned dog."

He heard her soothing Specter, and a moment later she unlocked the front door. He looked down at her, thinking she looked warm and familiar and altogether wonderful.

"What are you doing up at this time of night?" he asked, stepping into the hall.

"I was about to ask you the same question. Good grief, Colby, it's nearly two in the morning. What are you doing running around like this in the middle of the night?"

"Couldn't sleep. Thought I'd take a walk and I saw your light on." He shrugged out of the leather jacket he'd slung on before leaving the house. "No, that's not quite accurate. The truth is, I thought I'd take a walk and see if by any chance you'd open your door to me at two in the morning." He dropped the jacket on the hall table, pulled her close and kissed her heavily.

She looked up at him when he lifted his head. Her eyes were wide, her gaze surprisingly vulnerable. "To tell you the truth," Diana said softly, "I'm glad you came by."

He held her tightly for a long moment. "Rough day, huh? Those weeds really upset you, didn't they?"

"Yes."

"I promise you I'll find out who put them there, honey. And when I do, whoever did it will be eating small rocks off the pavement. Come on. Let's go into the kitchen and pour ourselves a medicinal glass of brandy."

"I just made some hot chocolate."

"That sounds even better."

They picked up their mugs and headed for the living room. Diana sat down beside him on the old couch, curling her legs under her. Specter lounged nearby, watchful as always, but apparently resigned to the fact that Colby had exerted his right to be here at this hour.

"Are horror writers subject to a lot of sleepless nights?" Diana asked as she sipped her hot chocolate.

Colby smiled faintly. "No, not really. At least I'm not. Not any more, at any rate. I used to lie awake a lot at night when I was a kid."

"Dreaming up stories?"

"Fighting monsters that hid in the closet. I'd imagine the most horrendous monster I could, and then I wouldn't be able to go to sleep until I'd also imagined how to destroy it."

"Sounds like a way of dealing with the trauma of your childhood."

She made the observation with such sweet, grave seriousness that Colby chuckled. "Don't tell me you're an amateur psychologist as well as a first-rate business executive."

She gave him a fleeting little smile. "Well, whatever the reason for inventing monsters, it's certainly stood you in good stead. When did you first start writing, Colby?"

"When Brandon started school, I went back, too, part-time. I enrolled in a local community college and, among other things, I wound up taking some writing classes. One of my teachers encouraged me to submit a couple of short stories, so I did. Nothing sold but I was hooked. I decided I wanted to write a book."

"Did you start off with horror?"

He shook his head, remembering the long, lean years. "No, I did a lot of men's action adventure stuff under a variety of names. Not much money in it, but eventually I worked it up to the point where I was earning almost as much writing as I was working in construction. That's when I quit and started writing full-time. That's also when I branched out into the horror market and started using my own name."

"A long, hard road."

His mouth curved reminiscently. "I was rather nervous the day I told my foreman I was quitting construction. I was sure that as soon as I gave up my real job, I'd stop selling books and then what would I do? After all, I had a responsibility to Brandon. But I took a chance, and I got lucky."

"Sometimes we have to make that kind of decision."

He sprawled back into the corner of the couch, pulling her with him. "Speaking of decisions, I get the impression Brandon is definitely pulling back from marriage. I owe you one for the advice you gave me, honey."

"Forget it. I hope they both come to realize marriage probably isn't the best thing for either of them at this age. From Robyn's point of view, especially, I think it would be a mistake."

"I gathered that." He tightened his arm around her. "You sure are big on women being able to take care of themselves, aren't you?"

"It's important to me."

"So important that you've never taken the risk of marriage or the risk of having kids."

Diana tensed. "Hey, don't you start in on me. Robyn's already given me a lecture on the subject of being an overly ambitious, tough, aggressive business-woman, remember?"

"So, why are you one?" Colby asked abruptly.

For an instant he thought he'd gone too far. She was utterly rigid beside him. "If that's the way you think of me, why are you here tonight?"

"Because I know that beneath all that ambition, toughness and aggression, you are one sexy lady who has a nifty way of driving me stark raving wild." He grinned unabashedly and kissed her soundly. "And any woman who looks as sweet and soft and tasty when she's wearing a robe and slippers as you do has defi-nitely got other talents besides her business skills. So tell me why you grew up thinking you could never rely on a man."

She lay still, looking up at him in surprise. "You're a little more perceptive than I would have guessed, Sav-agar."

"Don't look so astonished." He was mildly annoyed. "I'm not totally insensitive, you know. It was obvious from the way you lectured Robyn tonight that something has made you afraid to trust men. Was it just that guy who left you for his ex? Or is it all the lousy male bosses you've had over the years?"

"It's a lot of things, Colby. And it all boils down to a conviction that it's safer to rely on yourself. You can hardly argue with me on that score. You've got the same opinions on the subject."

"Yeah, you're right. Okay, in my case, it's probably because I've always felt that I was out there on my own. Aunt Jesse was hardly an anchor in a storm, and there's never been anyone else I could count on. I got used to taking care of myself. What about you?"

"A similar story. Except that I was lucky enough to have my mother. Dad took off when I was less than a year old. He never sent Mom a dime. Just disappeared. Poor Mom had gotten pregnant in high school and married without graduating. Her parents helped out but they didn't have much to spare. My mother has worked hard all her life, but you can imagine the kind of minimum-wage jobs she's had to take. There were Christmases when the only gift under the tree was the one she talked the Salvation Army into giving me."

"And you swore you were never going to get into that situation. You never wanted to take the risk of being financially dependent on a man."

"That's the long and the short of it."

"Did it occur to you that you may have carried your quest for independence to an extreme?" Colby asked dryly.

"I've been reasonably content. I'm in a position now where I have everything I want and I can afford to make my mother's life a lot easier."

"You told Robyn tonight that you can't always have it all."

"That's just being realistic. Life is often a series of trade-offs."

"Tell me something," Colby ordered softly. "Have you ever really trusted a man? Trusted him to take care of you? Trusted him to be strong for you? To be there for you?"

"Have you ever really trusted a woman that much?" she countered.

"No," he admitted somberly. *But I've never met a woman quite like you, before, either,* he thought.

"I think you understand me, Colby. We have some things in common, don't we?"

"Yes."

They were quiet together for a long while before they both fell asleep there on the lumpy old sofa.

9

DIANA AWOKE FEELING pleasantly crushed. It took her a few minutes to realize she was on the sofa, and that Colby was the crushing force that was being applied along the length of her.

"Beats waking up in a cave," Colby muttered without opening his eyes. At that moment, Specter stepped close to the sofa and put his damp nose against the first available chunk of warm human skin he found. He whined demandingly. Colby swore. "Tell that dog that if he wants to survive until nightfall, he'd better get his wet nose away from my back."

"I think he wants to go outside."

Colby opened one eye. "Then why don't you let him out?"

"Because you're on the outside of the sofa. It would be much easier for you to get up and let him out."

"There will be snow in August before I do that dog any favors. I've got more interesting things to do this morning." He slid a warm palm over the curve of Diana's hip.

"Letting him out first thing in the morning isn't exactly a favor. It's more of a necessity."

Specter emphasized the point with another sharp whine. He moved his cold nose up the length of Colby's spine, pushing the rumpled khaki shirt out of the way as he went.

"All right, all right. I surrender. I can take anything but wet-dog-nose torture." Colby rolled to his feet and stretched hugely. "Come on, you great slobbering beast. Outside. I may use you in a book one of these days, you know that?"

Specter leaped forward enthusiastically. Diana listened to the front door open and close and thought about how nice it was to have the man she loved waking up with her in the mornings. A woman could get addicted to this special kind of luxury. It would be dangerous to indulge herself too much.

She opened her eyes to find Colby standing beside the sofa, shedding the jeans in which he had slept. Dawn light danced on his powerful, naked shoulders. There was a possessive intentness in his gaze that sent small shock waves through her nerve endings.

For an instant, time went still in that strange way that it did sometimes when she was with Colby. She saw the fathomless desire etched in the hard lines of his face and felt the waves of his fierce will lapping at her. *He was so strong, a legendary warrior, a man who dominated everything and everyone around him.* She was suddenly overwhelmed with the knowledge that she was engaged in a battle.

She was caught, trapped, *chained* . . .

And then Colby was grinning down at her, gray eyes warm and lazy with early-morning sensuality.

Yes, he was dangerous, she thought. But how could she resist? Diana opened her arms to him, and he came to her at once.

A LONG TIME LATER, Colby again rolled off the couch, this time rubbing his bristly jaw. "Too bad I forgot to bring along a razor. I wouldn't have this problem if you were living with me."

"You can use mine."

"I think I'll just do that. Serve you right for being too stubborn to move in with me. And then we'll fix breakfast, and then I have got to get some work done today. What with one thing and another, I'm not exactly producing pages of manuscript lately. I think I'll kick the kids out of the house for the day, lock all the doors, make a large pot of coffee and spend some time doing what I'm supposed to be doing this summer."

"Colby?"

"Hmm?"

"I'm glad you came by when you did last night. It would have been a very long night, otherwise."

He leaned down and gathered her up into his arms, crushing her very close once more. "I'm glad you needed me a little last night. Because I needed you, too."

She clung to him until Specter scratched at the front door.

THREE HOURS LATER, Brandon appeared in the Jeep. Specter raced out ferociously at the familiar sound of the engine, but when he saw who was at the wheel he immediately lost interest in the attack.

"Hi, Diana," Brandon said when Diana walked out onto the porch. "Dad won't let anyone into the house. He says Robyn and I are supposed to entertain ourselves for the day. We've already gone hiking, and now Robyn is reading out there under the trees. I'm on my way into town to pick up Dad's mail and some groceries. Dad said you might want to go along. He said you usually go into town about this time, too."

"That sounds great, Brandon. I'll get my bag."

"Specter can come, too," Brandon called after her. "That's why I brought the Jeep. There's room for both of you."

"If only your father were so gracious toward my dog. Specter might take an entirely different attitude toward him."

Brandon laughed, and a few minutes later the Jeep pulled out of the yard with all of them aboard.

"You drive like your father," Diana muttered as Brandon whipped the Jeep neatly into a curve and accelerated confidently on the other side. The sense of speed, power and control was very familiar.

"Probably because he taught me," Brandon said with a casual shrug. "Specter okay back there?"

"He's fine." Diana patted Specter, who had his nose stuck out into the slipstream.

There were several interested stares as Brandon parked the Jeep in front of the post office. Across the street, Eddy Spooner waved from under the hood of a car. Diana waved back on the way into the gossip center of Fulbrook Corners.

"Groceries next," she announced a few minutes later when they trooped back out of the post office.

"I'll come with you," Brandon said. "Got to get some stuff for dinner. Dad says we're having you over again tonight." He glanced around with interest. "Hard to believe Dad grew up in a place like this. Somehow it just doesn't look like him."

"I don't think he fit in too well here," Diana murmured.

"I wonder why he came back this summer."

"It's an interesting question."

It was then that Diana saw the aging blue Cadillac moving ponderously down the street toward them. She knew in that moment that she faced a major decision. She also knew there weren't many options. The Cadillac was already slowing in front of them. Harry was going to park in front of the grocery store.

"Brandon?"

"Yeah, Diana?"

"That's your grandmother in the Cadillac."

Brandon came to an abrupt halt, staring in fascination as Harry got out of the car and opened the door for the regal woman inside. Margaret Fulbrook stood waiting, her eyes riveted on her grandson.

"Good morning, Mrs. Fulbrook," Diana said quietly as she and Brandon drew close. "Allow me to present Brandon Savagar. Brandon, this is Margaret Fulbrook." She held her breath, but Brandon's innate good manners overcame the traumatic nature of the moment.

"How do you do, Mrs. Fulbrook?" he said with admirable calm.

"You look like him," Margaret Fulbrook snapped accusingly. "Just like he did at your age. Except for the eyes. What they told me about your eyes is true. They're just like Cynthia's."

"That's what Dad always said."

"I'm surprised your father would admit there was any part of you that resembled your mother's side of the family. What did Colby tell you about Cynthia when you were growing up?"

"He said she was very pretty."

Margaret Fulbrook's eyes softened reminiscently. "Yes," she said, "my daughter was very pretty. Very full of life. If it hadn't been for your father..."

Brandon didn't wait for her to finish. "Excuse me, Mrs. Fulbrook. We've got some shopping to do." He took Diana's arm with all the cool aplomb Colby would have demonstrated in the situation and started toward the entrance of the grocery store. Diana didn't try to stop him.

"Where do you think you're going, young man?" Margaret Fulbrook shrilled behind them. "You come back here this instant. I'm talking to you. Harry, stop him. Stop him this instant."

Harry lumbered into their path, moving as heavily as the big Cadillac he drove. His small eyes were narrowed in anticipation. "You heard her, kid. She wants to talk to you. Do like she says, or I'll give you what I gave your father one night, back when he was your age."

Brandon released Diana's arm. She could feel him preparing himself.

"Don't worry, Brandon," she said smoothly, "your father says Harry's big, but he's slow. And if he was too slow to take your father twenty years ago, I think it's safe to assume that by now poor Harry's turned into molasses."

Rage creased Harry's heavy face. "Slow, am I? I'll show you who's slow." He raised a meaty fist, glaring at Brandon. "You're just like him, damn you. Just like him. He probably taught you a couple of his sucker punches. But I'll take you. See if I don't."

Brandon stood waiting. He never took his eyes off his opponent.

Diana turned to fix Margaret Fulbrook with a withering glance. "This little performance is certainly guaranteed to make sure Brandon never speaks to you again, isn't it, Mrs. Fulbrook?"

"I want to talk to him. I must talk to him. Now that I've seen him, I must speak to him. Don't you understand?"

"I understand. But the first requirement is that you call off Harry." Diana was aware of the gathering ring of onlookers. "If there's bloodshed, this will be the end of it, Mrs. Fulbrook. You'll never see Brandon again."

"But he was leaving," Mrs. Fulbrook wailed. "I was trying to talk to him and he walked away from me."

"Only because you started to bad-mouth Dad," Brandon said, still not looking away from Harry. "I'm willing to talk to you, ma'am, but I won't let you say anything against my father."

There was an acute silence and then Margaret Fulbrook heaved a deep sigh. "Come away from him, Harry."

"But, Mrs. Fulbrook . . ."

"I said, come away from him."

Harry was clearly vastly disappointed, but he obeyed reluctantly.

"Now come back here and talk to me, boy."

Brandon turned around slowly. "You give me your word you won't criticize Dad?"

"It will be hard not to criticize him," Mrs. Fulbrook said honestly. "I've had twenty years of practice. But I'll do my best. Now come over here and let me look at those eyes again."

Diana smiled slightly as Brandon went back toward his grandmother. "I'll do the grocery shopping while you two go have a cup of coffee," she said.

But neither Brandon nor Margaret Fulbrook were paying her any attention. They were too busy looking at each other's eyes.

AN HOUR LATER, a thoughtful Brandon dropped Diana and Specter off at the cottage. Brandon had said little on the way back from town, but when Diana started to climb out of the Jeep he spoke.

"What do you think of her, Diana?"

She sat back in the seat and studied Brandon's intent, concerned expression. "She's a bitter old woman who has denied herself her grandson for twenty years. Now she's seen you and she's regretting having let all that time go by. You're all she has left."

"I felt kind of sorry for her. In spite of the way she sicced old Harry on us."

"You were generous and kind to her today, Brandon. You gave her something she could never have bought, or stolen, or taken by force. Deep down she knows that." Impulsively Diana leaned across the seat and kissed him lightly on the cheek. "Only a real man could have handled that situation as well as you did today. I'm proud to know you." She backed out of the Jeep. Specter jumped down beside her and immediately headed for the porch steps.

"Diana, wait." Brandon had turned brick red at her comment on his manliness, but he looked very pleased. "What do you think I should tell Dad?"

"I don't know. The truth, I suppose. He must have known that with you in town the meeting was inevitable. I think his main concern was that Mrs. Fulbrook would try to hurt you somehow. But when he realizes how well you handled the whole thing, he'll relax. And you did handle it well, Brandon. You had her eating out of the palm of your hand."

Brandon grinned. "Not quite, but she's certainly not the tough old bird Dad made her out to be."

"Maybe she was a lot tougher twenty years ago."

Brandon put the Jeep in gear. "Probably. See you later, Diana, and thanks."

Diana watched him wheel the Jeep out of the drive, and then she turned toward the cottage. "Come on, Specter, old buddy, let's get ourselves a snack."

But for once Specter did not come to instant attention at the mention of food. He was sniffing around the front door and making odd snuffling sounds.

Diana felt chilled. "Specter? What is it? What's wrong?" She dug her keys out of her shoulder bag and started to fit them into the front door. Specter scratched at the screen, obviously impatient.

Maybe Colby was inside, Diana thought. But why hadn't he come out when he heard the Jeep? She turned the key slowly and then instinctively stood back to let the dog enter first.

Specter didn't hesitate. He trotted inside and began sniffing around the hall table. Diana followed slowly, trying to figure out what was so wrong in the hallway.

It took her a full three seconds to realize the small table with the empty vase was positioned on the left side of the hall instead of the right.

Someone had moved it. Someone who had studied *Shock Value*.

"My God, Specter. Someone's deliberately spooking me. Someone's trying to scare the daylights out of me."

Whoever he was, he was succeeding.

Diana stared at the hall table for a few more seconds, aware of her pounding pulse and the cold dampness of her own nervous sweat. She tried to think clearly. The intruder must have long since departed, she assured herself. Specter would not be this calm if there was someone hiding in the cottage.

She made herself walk past the table into the kitchen. This time she didn't have to search through her copy of *Shock Value* to find the pertinent passage. The book was lying open on the table. Diana gazed down at page fifty-six. For a moment she couldn't seem to focus. Then the words settled into place on the page.

It was such a small thing, this new position of the table, just a minor adjustment in his everyday world. It was the kind of casual rearrangement of furniture that anyone might try, to see if the space could be better utilized or if eye appeal could be enhanced.

But the effect was devastating. Some minor demon had paused long enough in Donnelly's personal universe to introduce an element of horrific chaos.

Because Donnelly knew that no human hand could have moved the table. There was no way anyone could have entered the house undetected. The security system he'd installed was foolproof.

But he refused to believe in demons, minor or otherwise.

Perhaps the time had come to ask himself if he was going insane. It would be interesting to see what the verdict was.

Diana couldn't bring herself to read any further. She closed the book and went slowly into the living room. Specter had lost interest in the table. He followed his mistress and flopped at her feet when she sank down onto the sofa.

Diana was still huddled on the sofa half an hour later when the Jeep roared back into her drive. Specter raised his head and barked ferociously.

Relief flooded through Diana when she realized it had to be Colby. It was a shock to acknowledge to herself how much she needed him in that moment, needed to turn to him for comfort and reassurance, needed him for his strength and the protection he could provide. It was the first time in her life she had ever considered turning to a man for such things. But then, she had never known a man like Colby.

Then she heard the screen door slam with sickening fury and Diana's relief turned to dread. The last thing she needed right now was Colby's anger.

Sensing genuine rage, Specter changed his familiar growl of protest into something much more serious. But Colby ignored the dog. He came down the hall in three long strides, and his glittering eyes went straight to Diana. His face was a mask of hard fury as he came toward her.

For an instant Diana felt as if she had slipped back into an ancient past to face an implacable male. *The warrior's anger was fully aroused. He would not tol-*

erate her defiance. He would not rest until he had sub-
dued her.

"You couldn't resist, could you?" Colby stopped in
front of her and hauled her to her feet. "You just could
not resist. I told you to stay out of it. He's my son, god-
damn it. *My* son. And you knew I didn't want him
meeting that old bitch. Damn you, Diana. You had no
right to get involved. No *right*. Who the hell do you
think you are?"

It was too much to deal with. Coming on top of the
shock she'd had earlier, Colby's fury was too much.
This was always the way it was. When the chips were
down, you could depend on no one but yourself. A
woman could not afford to rely on a man. Only a fool
would believe that any man would be there when you
needed him.

"Let me go, Colby." Her voice was low and tight.
Specter crowded close, teeth showing.

"You deliberately set it up for them to meet, didn't
you? You went behind my back and planned the whole
thing."

"No, Colby, I didn't plan it. It just happened."

"The hell it did. It wouldn't have happened if I'd been
there, you can bet on that. Christ, lady, you introduced them. Brandon told me exactly how it worked.
You introduced my son to that old she-devil who has
totally ignored him for nearly twenty years. I trusted
you, damn it. I thought you were on my side. It never
occurred to me you'd go behind my back like this."

Diana strove to keep her face expressionless. His
hands were like steel clamps on her arms. She looked
up at him and knew that it was hopeless. "I'm sorry,
Colby."

"Sure you are," he bit out scathingly. "I'll tell you who's sorry. I'm the one who's sorry. Sorry for trusting you. Sorry for believing you were different from other women. I was a fool, but it was my son who paid the price of my damned idiocy." He released her with an angry gesture and stalked to the window. "I don't know what the hell made me think I could trust you just because you're good in bed."

Diana wrapped her arms around herself, withdrawing from Colby's anger and the insult he'd offered. Specter huddled closer, whining softly. His massive body was a source of comfort in the storm. She could feel the tension in him. It occurred to her that Specter was the one male on earth she could rely upon.

"He bought her a cup of coffee. Can you believe it?" Colby slammed the palm of his hand against the windowsill. "He bought Margaret Fulbrook a cup of coffee and sat there talking to her while you blithely went grocery shopping."

"Colby..."

"I heard she sicced that stupid ox, Harry, on the two of you. Tell me, what would you have done if that creep had taken a swing at my son? How would you have felt then?"

"Brandon handled him very well. There was no fight."

"No thanks to you. You must have thought you were being so damned clever." Colby raked his hand through his hair in his characteristic gesture.

"You've said enough, Colby."

Her low, cold, utterly formal tone seemed to get through to him. His head came around swiftly and he gave her a seething look.

"What don't you want to hear?" he asked far too softly. "That you're so accustomed to playing lady executive that you can't resist the opportunity to power-trip in someone else's life? That you think you're smarter than anyone else? That you're better equipped than others to make the kind of decisions that will affect people for years to come?"

"Colby, I said that's enough. I get the point. I think it's time you left." It took every ounce of her self-control to hold herself in check. She wanted to cry—to scream abuse at him for not being there for her when she needed him. But if she had learned anything in the business world, it was how to control her outward emotions around a man.

"I've got a lot more to say to you, lady."

She closed her eyes, clutching herself more tightly, holding herself together as she had always held herself together in front of others. "You probably do, but I'd rather not hear it. Now will you please go away, Colby? You've told me what you thought of me. I swear I won't get involved with you or Brandon again. You have my word of honor."

"What the hell is your word of honor worth?"

Diana opened her eyes and looked straight into his smoky gaze. "Believe me, Colby, in this case, you may rely on it completely. If you like, I'll give you a money-back guarantee that I won't see either you or your son again. Now will you leave?"

Specter reinforced the quiet command with a rumbling growl. He stood braced at Diana's feet.

"Yeah, I'll leave, Diana." Colby started past her toward the door. "You've done enough damage. No point hanging around to see what other tricks you've got up your sleeve."

He slammed the screen door more loudly on the way out than he had on the way in.

"He didn't even notice the hall table," Diana observed to her dog. Then she sank back down onto the sofa and let the pent-up tears flow.

THE MOST FRUSTRATING THING had been watching her withdraw into herself. She had reacted to him as if he had been some wild, dangerous force of nature. She had battened down the hatches, erected the barriers that would keep her safe and secure and then stood there and let him rage.

She had handled him the way she probably handled every other male in her life. She had retreated behind that cool, collected, untouchable facade and waited for him to do his worst.

He realized he had wanted her to react somehow. He wished she had cried, or shouted, or pounded on him with her small fists. Anything would have been preferable to that cool retreat.

He'd been angry and she was to blame. Colby had wanted a fight, and she had refused to enter the lists. That riled him as much as the original reason for his anger.

Colby snapped the Jeep around the last hairpin turn in River Road and then slowed the vehicle and turned into the parking area below Chained Lady Falls. He switched off the ignition with a violent twist and then sat, arms braced on the wheel, staring at the foaming water pouring down the cliff.

*She'd had no right to introduce Brandon to the old
bitch.*

Brandon had claimed that Margaret Fulbrook had
obviously engineered the meeting, but Colby knew it
could have been avoided. All Diana and Brandon had
to do was perform a simple hundred and eighty degree
turn, get back in the Jeep and drive away. But, no.
Diana had calmly made introductions and then sent
Brandon off to have a cup of coffee with his grandmother.

His son had shared a cup of coffee with the old bat.
Colby still couldn't believe it. And Diana had coolly
done the grocery shopping while Brandon dealt with
Margaret Fulbrook alone. It was too much. Too
damned much.

What if Harry had swung at Brandon? It was true
Colby had made certain Brandon was trained to take
care of himself, but the boy had never been in a real
street fight.

Harry was slow, but vicious and strong. One lucky
punch was all it would have taken to down Brandon.
What if Diana had gotten caught in the middle of such
a fight? Not an unlikely possibility since she probably
would have tried to stop it. She would have been seriously injured.

Colby's right hand clenched into a fist. He forced
himself to relax the fingers one at a time. There was no
excuse for Diana's behavior. She had known full well
that he hadn't wanted Brandon to meet Margaret Fulbrook.

Sure, Brandon had been curious about his grandmother, but the boy wouldn't have engineered the

meeting against Colby's direct orders. It was Diana who had taken it upon herself to arrange it.

"Damn it to hell."

He should never have come back here this summer. Everything would have been fine if he hadn't taken it into his head to see Fulbrook Corners again. He must have been out of his mind.

But if he hadn't come back here, he would never have met Diana.

Colby got out of the Jeep and walked to the edge of the water. Mist from the falls enveloped him, dampening his hair and his shirt. He stood looking up toward the hidden cave.

She had been so warm and loving and sweet that night. She had been everything he'd ever wanted in a woman. She had given herself to him in a way he knew instinctively she had never given herself to any other man. She had held back nothing. She had been his.

And the next morning she had acted as though nothing had happened, even though there was a very real chance she might have gotten pregnant.

Today she had given him her personal, money-back guarantee that she wouldn't involve herself in his life ever again. She was going to walk away from him the way she planned to walk away from her job. Probably saw herself as a victim of male chauvinism once more.

Colby turned back to the Jeep and got behind the wheel. He didn't like the idea that she was lumping him in with every other unreliable male in her life—her father, the men she worked for, that bastard when she was twenty-five.

But he had a right to his anger, by God. It was she who had failed him, not the other way around. She had no business going cold and brittle on him the way she had when he'd yelled at her. No business withdrawing into herself like that.

He was half way back to Aunt Jesse's before he began to calm down and think rationally.

The first rational thought that occurred to him was that he couldn't let Diana just walk out of his life.

The second rational thought was that there had been something wrong with the hall table in her cottage.

10

DIANA HAD FINISHED cleaning up the kitchen and was packing unused food into a cooler when Specter snarled a warning. A moment later she heard the Jeep engine and closed her eyes in pain. Colby was back to yell at her again. Diana didn't think she could take any more.

She straightened and went quickly down the hall to the front door. She managed to set the lock just as he vaulted up the steps to the front porch. He must have heard the faint click.

"Diana, let me in." Colby pounded peremptorily on the door.

Specter barked loudly in response, but Diana didn't bother to answer. She went back down the hall to the kitchen, locked the back door and then resumed her packing.

The pounding continued. "Damn it, Diana, let me in. I've got to talk to you."

Diana let Specter answer for her. The dog did so enthusiastically. The ensuing racket of barking and fist-pounding continued unabated for a couple of minutes. The pounding stopped first. Specter gave one last victorious woof and trotted into the kitchen.

"Good dog," Diana murmured. "I can count on you, at least, can't I?"

But there was no sound of the Jeep's engine being switched on, and Specter began to growl again. He stood poised for a moment and then, with a loud yelp, went dashing out of the kitchen toward the bedroom.

"Too late, you fool dog. I'm already inside."

Colby's voice came from the bedroom and Diana remembered the window she had left open in there. She turned slowly around to face him as he strode into the kitchen. Specter growled at his heels but made no move to cause genuine injury.

"What the hell is going on here?" Colby demanded, taking in the array of boxes and cleaning items.

"What does it look like? I'm getting ready to leave." Diana made herself go back to work, methodically putting packaged food items into a box to take with her.

"Going to run out now after causing all the trouble?" he asked, his voice rough.

"I gave you my word I would not interfere in your life again, Colby. That means I have to leave Fulbrook Corners. To use an old western expression, this town isn't big enough for both of us. There's no way we can avoid running into each other here."

"Do you always run away when things don't work out the way you had planned?"

"As I told Brandon the other night at dinner, a smart businesswoman has to know when to cut her losses."

"And I'm a loss, is that it?"

She took a firm grasp on her jangled nerves and uncertain temper. "The bottom line is that our *relationship* is a loss. A complete write-off."

He walked over to a kitchen chair, spun it around and straddled it backward. He crossed his arms along the laddered seat back and watched her with brooding eyes. "Is it comfortable and convenient to be able to talk about our relationship in business jargon? It's a complete write-off? It's time to cut your losses? Let me tell you something, the bottom line as far as I'm concerned is that I don't like being referred to as just another bad business investment."

Diana's hands tightened on a box of cereal until the thin cardboard began to crumple. "You're the creative writer in the crowd. You think of a better way to put it."

"Okay, how's this? You're a coward, Diana. You think that when the going gets tough, tough ladies like you can just walk away from the problem."

Her head came up sharply as anger surged through her. "That's nonsense and you know it. You're the one who ended this so-called relationship, not me. You marched in here a little while ago and told me I was an interfering, manipulative troublemaker."

"You were. And I was madder than hell."

"Is that right? Well, so am I. Why don't you just get out of here, Colby? Go on, get lost. I've got work to do."

"You can't run away from me."

"Who's going to stop me?"

"I am," Colby said bluntly.

"You're not making sense. Less than an hour ago you were telling me to stay out of your life."

"I never said that."

"Well, that's what it sounded like to me."

"I told you, I was angry," Colby said through his teeth. "And with good reason. I did not, however, kick you out of my life."

"Close enough."

"And you decided I was just like every other man you've ever known, didn't you?" he shot back swiftly and softly. "But you're wrong. I'll admit I can see where you got that impression about me, though."

"Is that right?"

"You needed me. You were probably scared to death, and all I did was rage at you and then storm out the door. A lot of sound and fury, but not particularly useful when the crunch came. Is that what all the men in your life have been like, Diana?"

"I was not frightened of you," she said with great dignity. "I have never been frightened of any man."

"Is that right? You were frightened of whoever moved that table in your hall."

She dropped the bottle of mustard she had been about to place in the box. For an instant there was silence.

"I didn't think you'd noticed," Diana said at last, not looking at him.

"I was too damned mad to notice it right away. But then I drove out to Chained Lady Falls to think, and after a while I remembered there was something different about the hall table. Something that reminded me of a scene out of one of my books."

"*Shock Value*. Page fifty-six."

Colby nodded slowly, his eyes never leaving hers. "When did it happen?"

"The table being moved? I don't know. While Brandon and I were in town, I guess. It was like that when I got back."

"It was a shock, wasn't it?"

"That's putting it mildly. Someone around here doesn't like me, Colby. And your theory that it might be Margaret Fulbrook is wrong. She was having coffee with Brandon while my table was being moved."

Colby eye's narrowed. "Harry could have done it."

"No. Harry sat out in the Cadillac the whole time Brandon and Margaret were in the café."

"That leaves a town full of possibilities," Colby mused.

"Well, whoever did it will have to find a new hobby. I'll be safely back in Portland tonight."

"You'll be safely over at Aunt Jesse's place tonight," Colby said flatly.

Diana eyed him warily. "No, thanks. I've had enough of Fulbrook Corners."

"And enough of me, is that it?"

"To be perfectly frank, dealing with a nasty prankster and a man who thinks I've committed the ultimate act of disloyalty is a bit much to handle. Even for me."

"You didn't commit the ultimate act of disloyalty," Colby muttered. "Just a minor indiscretion. The ultimate act of disloyalty would be for you to sleep with another man."

"I can't tell you how relieved I am to hear that my sin was not a mortal one. Will you please go away and let me pack?"

He didn't move. "Diana, I had a right to be furious with you."

She shrugged, pulling more items out of the cupboard. "Maybe. It's a matter of opinion. Your son wanted to meet his grandmother. He's an adult and he has some rights, too, you know. When I saw her standing there on the street, staring at him, I simply made the introductions. As far as I was concerned, the issue was Brandon's to decide. Not yours and not mine."

Colby drew a deep breath. "Maybe that's why I was so mad," he said slowly. "Maybe I didn't want to admit that the decision was Brandon's. I told you I've made a lot of mistakes as a father. No reason to think I'm not capable of making a few more."

"Tell Brandon that. I'm sure he'll understand. He's a very sensitive, understanding young man."

"Unlike his father?"

"You're a lot more cynical than he is, but then, you went through a far tougher childhood and adolescence. And don't be too hard on yourself, Colby. You're the one responsible for turning Brandon into the fine young man he is. Now, if you'll excuse me, I want to finish this packing."

"Diana, you're coming over to my place for the night. You'll be safe there."

"I'll be safer in Portland."

There was a loud crash as Colby shot to his feet and sent the chair spinning backward against the wall. "Damn you, you stubborn, thickheaded, self-contained female. You don't think you can even rely on me enough to let me protect you, do you?"

Diana clenched her hands to stop her fingers from trembling. "Why should you want to protect me?"

"Because you belong to me. Haven't you figured that much out yet?"

"You mean because we started a brief summer affair you feel you have some responsibility toward me?" she mocked. "Forget it, Colby. I can take care of myself. I've been doing it a long time now. Besides, the affair is over. Your sense of obligation can take a hike."

He reached her in two long strides and caught her deftly by the nape of the neck. His touch was astonishingly gentle but there was too much strength in his hand for her to successfully resist him. His eyes softened a little as he looked down at her. "The affair is a long way from over and you know it. As for my sense of obligation, we can discuss that later. At Aunt Jesse's place. Don't fight me on this, honey. You know I'll go out of my mind if I have to worry about you staying here alone, and I can't let you drive back to Portland. Not yet. There's too much between us."

"Is there?" She could hardly get the words out. She was ensnared in his glittering, determined gazed.

"Yes," Colby stated. "There is."

The fact that he understood that much was what made Diana keep her mouth shut as she went down the hall to get her overnight things.

"DAD BLEW UP when I told him about meeting Grandmother today," Brandon said an hour later. He and Diana were sitting in two of the decrepit chairs on the porch of Aunt Jesse's old house. Robyn was upstairs sulking, and Colby had gone back to work. "But he's seriously angry about these stupid pranks someone's playing on you."

Diana sipped iced tea and regarded her companion with a skeptical expression. "Seriously angry? You think he's more annoyed because of the pranks than he is because I introduced you to Margaret Fulbrook?"

"Definitely."

"I think you've got that backward. Colby's not happy about the pranks, but I would say that he was definitely, seriously angry about your meeting your grandmother."

"Nah. You don't know Dad as well as I do. When he starts yelling, he's mad, all right. But he cools down after he's let off steam. On the other hand, when he gets quiet, that's when you know you've got a problem."

"I'll try to keep the distinction in mind," Diana said with a wry smile.

"Were you really on your way back to Portland?"

"Yes."

"Dad must have come unglued."

"No," Diana said reflectively. "He just got madder."

"I'm glad you didn't go. He's really hung up on you, you know."

"No, I don't know. I can't always figure your father out, Brandon."

"Most people can't. I know him better than anyone, and I still have problems figuring him out at times. But he's okay when the chips are down, you know what I mean? He takes care of things."

"I think you're a lot like him in that respect, Brandon," Diana said gently. She was about to say something else but Robyn wandered out onto the porch at that moment. The young woman gave Diana a baleful glance and turned to Brandon.

"I'm bored. There's nothing to do around here. You want to take a walk or something, Brandon? I need to talk to you."

"Sure." Brandon got to his feet. "See you later, Diana. Want to come along, Specter?" He slapped his thigh encouragingly.

Specter lumbered to his feet and cast a questioning glance at Diana.

"Go on," she said to the dog. "I'll be fine."

Specter trotted happily along after the pair, his shaggy tail waving cheerfully.

"Look at that fool dog," Colby said through the screen door. "Acts like he and Brandon have been best buddies for years. While I, on the other hand, get treated to bared teeth and salivating jaws."

"I guess something about you just irritates him," Diana said as she poured herself more iced tea and watched Brandon and Robyn disappear into the woods. "Do you want some tea?"

"Thanks." He pushed open the screen door, walked out onto the porch and dropped into the chair Brandon had been using. He took the cold glass from her hand and gazed after Brandon and Robyn. "I get the feeling dear little Robyn has about had it with Fulbrook Corners."

"I can empathize."

"You still mad at me?"

Diana thought about it. "Yes."

"You'll get over it."

"You think so?"

"Sure. I got over being mad at you, didn't I?" Colby pointed out with unarguable masculine logic.

"Did you?"

"Yes, damn it, I did." Colby set down his glass and reached over to snag her arm. He deftly removed the glass from her hand and pulled her out of her chair and across his lap. "Now stop trying to provoke me."

"What is this? You get to be mad as long as you like, but as soon as you're finished everyone else is supposed to go back to normal, too?"

"Works better that way." He cradled her close, his hand on her thigh, his lips in her hair.

"Colby, I want to talk to you."

"Talk fast." His hand traveled up her jean-clad thigh and settled on her hip.

"I don't think you've given this whole situation much thought."

"What situation?" His lips were on her throat.

Diana shivered and touched his shoulder longingly. "Me. Here in the house."

"As long as I'm willing to tolerate that stupid mutt of yours underfoot, where's the problem?"

"Well, the sleeping arrangements for one thing. Do you have a fourth bedroom?"

"Nope. Only got three."

"That's what I thought. So where am I supposed to sleep?"

He drew back for an instant to look down at her with genuine surprise. "You sleep with me, naturally. Where did you think you were going to sleep?"

"But what about the kids? Do you think they ought to see us, uh, going off to bed together?"

"As you and my son have both taken pains to point out to me lately, Brandon is no longer a kid. He already knows I'm sleeping with you and he approves. What more do you want?"

"What about Robyn?" Diana asked anxiously.

"If she's old enough to sleep with Brandon, she's old enough to handle the concept of a couple of genuine, grown-up adults sleeping together. Now stop worrying about it. The decision has already been made."

"By you?"

"Yeah. By me." His hand slid up just under her breast, his thumb sliding into her cleavage. "Now, tell me what you picked up for dinner tonight."

"I can't seem to remember at the moment. All I can think about is dessert." She smiled up at him, her fingertips trailing teasingly down the front of his shirt to the waistband of his jeans.

He grinned. "Does this mean I'm forgiven?"

"It means I'm prepared to let you prove just how remorseful you really are."

"Good idea. I'll start proving it right now."

Diana laughed and caught his exploring hand. "No, you will not. It's almost time to start dinner, and Brandon and Robyn will be back soon."

Colby muttered something under his breath and wrapped her so tightly to him that she squeaked. The sexy laughter faded from his eyes to be replaced with something more intense. "I think we can safely say we got though our first major quarrel today."

"Is that something to celebrate?"

"Yeah," he said. "I think it is. With any luck, you learned a few things today."

She gave him an indignant glare. "I learned a few things? What was I supposed to learn?"

His gaze was brilliant and grimly intent. "That I won't let you walk out of my life just because of a disagreement. Remember that, Diana."

She said nothing, touching his hard jaw with her forefinger in an unconsciously gentle action. Privately she wondered what it would take for him to let her walk out of his life.

Would he let her go if it turned out she was pregnant?

COLBY WAITED UNTIL Brandon and Robyn were deeply involved in a board game that night before he took Diana's hand and led her toward the stairs.

"Good night, you two. See you in the morning," he said as he started upstairs with Diana in tow.

Brandon looked up from the board and smiled at Diana. "Good night."

Robyn looked up briefly but said nothing. She had said very little all evening.

At the top of the stairs Diana said softly, "I don't think that girl likes me."

"Don't worry about it. I'm the one who has cause for worry. The thought of having her for a daughter-in-law sends chills down my spine."

"I think Brandon has definitely postponed thoughts of marriage. But I'm not so sure about Robyn. She really wants to get married, and she doesn't like being asked to wait."

"I just hope she doesn't do something really stupid like get pregnant."

Beside him, Diana fell silent. Too late he realized the stupidity of his last remark. Diana, of course, would take it personally. If she was pregnant . . .

Damn, but women were complicated creatures.

Colby opened the door of his bedroom and urged her inside. A surge of possessiveness and satisfaction went through him as he closed the door and watched her standing in the middle of his very personal domain. He leaned back against the door and drank his fill of her as she wandered curiously to the window, over to the dresser and then to the bed.

"Was this your room as a child?" she asked as she touched a model of a Corvette he had once painstakingly built from a kit.

Colby nodded. "Yeah."

She examined the model car. "It's hard to imagine you as a little kid."

He shrugged. "My big dream, aside from escaping Fulbrook Corners, was to own a 'vette."

"Did you ever get one?"

"Senior year in high school. A used one. Got it for a song because some guy had crashed it. Eddy helped me work on it. By the time we were finished, it was a teenager's dream. Black as midnight and faster than a bat out of hell. I beat everything I ever went up against out on River Road in that car. It was the pride and joy of my life."

"What happened to it?"

"I had a great time with it for a while." He took the model from her hand and studied it with a reminiscent smile. Then he shrugged and put the little 'vette down on a shelf. "Then I got married, and Brandon came along and I needed money for baby food and diapers and all the other things that a baby needs."

"So you sold your pride and joy?"

Colby laughed softly and walked over to sink down beside her. "Don't look so sad. It was a long time ago."

"And now you drive a Jeep?"

"I like to take it off-roading. A man's taste changes as he gets older." Colby leaned over her, easing her back onto the pillows and caging her with his hands. "Take you, for instance. I'm not sure I would have had the brains or the sense to properly appreciate you when I was nineteen. But now..." He kissed her slowly, deeply, giving her time to respond.

"And now?" she whispered huskily when he finally freed her mouth.

"Now I'm a lot older and wiser. And boy, do I appreciate you...."

Colby bent his head to kiss her again, and when she opened her mouth for him he slid his knee between her thighs. Diana's hand curved around his buttocks, urging him more tightly against her softness and she lifted her hips against his.

"I love the way you get so hot, so fast for me, honey. You make me crazy."

"I'm the one who goes crazy," she whispered, guiding his head down to her breasts. She was already unbuttoning her shirt for him, freeing herself of her peach-colored bra. "You make me ache all over, do you know that, Colby?"

And then she was offering her breasts to him, demanding and pleading for his intimate attention. Colby felt his already taut body ignite. The knowledge that she needed him, wanted him, would give herself to him whenever he turned to her was almost too much to handle. The growing realization that he had only to touch her to know she was his sent flames roaring through him.

He gently sucked one sweet, tight nipple between his teeth and simultaneously reached down to unfasten his jeans and then hers. Together they slithered out of the restricting clothing and then they were clinging to each other.

When Diana reached down to stroke the hardened length of his manhood, Colby nearly lost his self-control. She had a way of pushing him to the edge, and he loved it.

"Here," he muttered, scrabbling about in the night-stand drawer for the little foil packet. "You put it on."

"Me?"

"Yeah, you. I'll just lie here and go out of my mind."

She laughed softly and knelt beside him. Colby knew he'd made a serious error the minute he realized what a long production she was going to make out of the simple action. But the delicious sensations she created as she worked carefully and gently over him almost made up for the agony of waiting.

Almost.

The instant she was done, Diana sat back and examined her handiwork with satisfaction. "A perfect fit. Not bad, if I do say so myself."

Colby grinned, his teeth set as he struggled for self-control. "Come here and finish the job, you little witch."

She raised her brows mockingly. "I thought the job was finished."

"It's just started." He pulled her across his thighs, his hands clenching luxuriously into her hips. "Now show me just how perfect the fit really is."

Her eyes were bold and sensuous as she grasped him gently and began to ease him into her softness. He saw the glittering excitement in her, and it fed the flames of his own fire.

When she hesitated a little, teasing him unmercifully, Colby gave a soft, warning exclamation and then pulled her down abruptly, sinking himself to the hilt.

Diana bit back a gasp of excitement, and her head tipped back. She moved on him, setting the rhythm.

She guided his hands to where she wanted him to touch her and finally her whole body tightened.

When her lips parted, Colby quickly pulled her head down to his and stopped the delicious little screams with his mouth. He loved her beautiful cries of sensual surrender, but he knew she would be embarrassed later if she thought Brandon and Robyn had overheard.

Then he was exploding with her, gritting his teeth to stifle his own shout of satisfaction.

Together they drifted for a timeless moment. Colby kept his arms wrapped tightly around her, listening to her soft breathing and waiting for his body to glide back to normal.

"Now that's how I want every quarrel between us to end," he stated finally.

Diana stretched. "I've always heard you're not supposed to use sex to settle an argument."

"We settled it before we got into bed."

"Settled it?" Diana propped herself up on her elbows and glowered down at him. "That's what you call informing me that you're not mad any longer, and therefore the fight is hereby declared over?"

"Hey, I apologized, didn't I? Sort of?"

"You admitted you might have been a teeny-weeny bit out of line, but that's all."

He touched the tip of her nose with his forefinger. "I'll let you in on a little secret, sweetheart. That kind of admission is more than most people ever get out of me."

"Not used to admitting you might have overreacted, huh?"

"No. Because I generally don't overreact. Fulbrook Corners and Margaret Fulbrook in particular are two of the few things on earth that can make me overreact."

"So why are you here in Fulbrook Corners?"

"I wish to hell you'd stop asking me that question." Brandon's sense of satisfaction and well-being began to fade rapidly. "I've told you a dozen times why I'm here. Let's talk about something else before I get angry all over again."

She crossed her arms, leaning on his broad chest. "What would you like to talk about?"

"The fact that you didn't trust me to protect you from whoever is playing those pranks on you," he said coolly. "I think it's time you learned to trust me, Diana."

"I do trust you," she said seriously. "I wouldn't be sleeping with you if I didn't."

He shook his head. "When we argued earlier today, your immediate reaction was to pack and leave. That's not the kind of trust I had in mind."

"I thought things were over between us," she said stiffly.

"Well, they aren't," he growled.

"Trust works both ways, you know," she said quietly. "If you want me to trust you, I've got a right to expect trust in return."

Colby was silent for a long moment. "Just because I lost my temper with you today doesn't mean I don't trust you."

"Doesn't it?"

"No."

"Colby, I don't want to argue any more today. I've had enough."

He was instantly remorseful. "I know, baby, I know." He stroked her hair soothingly for a moment, but he was far from satisfied.

He knew now just how deeply ingrained her sense of independence and self-control were. When it came to dealing with men, she always went on the assumption that the male of the species could not be relied upon. So she'd learned how to take care of herself.

But it had become overwhelmingly important to get her to admit that he could take care of her.

Colby wondered how he was going to break through the last of her barriers. And he wondered if Diana realized how fast his own barriers were crumbling.

"What are you thinking, Colby?" Diana asked a long time later.

"You're supposed to be asleep." He cuddled her closer as she lay in the curve of his arm.

"So are you. What's keeping you awake?"

"I'm thinking about those damned pranks some idiot played on you."

"Any new ideas?"

"No, but I think I'll go out to Gil Thorp's place tomorrow. Eddy was no help, but Gil might have picked up a rumor or two. He used to be good at getting information." Colby grinned wryly in the darkness, remembering.

"Who's Gil Thorp?"

"He used to be the sheriff around here twenty years ago. He and I had what you might call an adversarial business relationship."

"What does that mean?"

"It means that every time I was conducting a little business out on River Road after midnight, Gil Thorp felt duty-bound to try to put a stop to it. Gil also didn't like the way I drove through town at twice the speed limit, or the way I got into fights, or the way I used to hang out with Eddy Spooner."

Diana shifted against him. "You don't sound as if you particularly dislike him."

"I don't dislike him. I told you, we had an adversarial relationship, but Thorp always played fair, unlike several other folks around here. And sometimes, after he'd interrupted a race and sent everyone home, he'd make me sit in that beat-up old patrol car of his and we'd talk. He had a way of getting me to tell him things I had never told anyone else. It was Gil who suggested I join the army."

"He became the closest thing to a father figure you ever had, is that it?"

"It wasn't exactly a close relationship, but he was there from time to time when I needed someone to tell me I'd gone too far or steer me clear of the kind of trouble that might have landed me in jail. One way or another, I probably owe Gil."

"Have you kept in touch?"

"Some. Christmas cards. A letter once in a while. Like I said, it wasn't really a close relationship. But he wasn't a half-bad cop, all things considered. He had a way of getting information. I'll check with him tomorrow."

"Colby?"

"Hmm?"

"One thing still doesn't make sense about those pranks."

"What?"

"The fact that they've been played against me, not you."

He stroked her arm. "Honey, I've told you, anyone who knows me would be able to figure out in a hurry that one of the fastest ways to get at me would be through you."

"I'm not so sure about that."

She didn't credit herself with enough power, he realized as he bent his head to kiss her. The woman was his weak spot, and she didn't even realize it. Maybe it was just as well. Women could be the very devil when they sensed they had real power over a man.

Colby wondered if he was becoming a weak spot for the self-controlled little amazon he held in his arms.

DIANA FOUND HERSELF at loose ends the next morning. Colby had taken the Jeep to go out to the Thorp ranch. Brandon and Robyn had gone on another hike, this time leaving Specter behind.

By eleven o'clock, Diana was worrying about the résumés she had planned to get in the mail that week.

"What do you say we walk over to the cottage, pick them up and take them into the post office, Specter?"

Specter was stretched out on the porch enjoying the morning sunlight. He didn't look overly enthusiastic about the prospect of a walk, but he obligingly got to his feet.

Fifteen minutes later Diana opened the door of her cottage with some trepidation. She acknowledged to herself that she was a little afraid of finding that another prank had been played in her absence.

"Colby probably would not approve of us coming back here alone," she informed the dog. "He seems to be very big on playing bodyguard these days."

Specter grunted, obviously unconcerned with Colby's approval. He bounded straight into the house without any sign of concern and headed for the kitchen. Diana walked in behind him and found the dog nosing around the cupboard where his biscuits were kept.

She fed him two crunchy tidbits and then went into the living room to stuff a few résumés and covering letters into envelopes. Half an hour later she was ready.

"Okay, boy, let's run these into town. If I don't find a good job by September, I'll be back at C and Y."

The trip into town was uneventful. Diana sent the résumés off with a silent prayer for good luck and headed her compact car back across the bridge toward Aunt Jesse's place. It was getting close to lunchtime. Brandon and Robyn would be hungry, and Colby might be back from visiting Gil Thorp.

She drove into the yard and parked the car. Specter jumped out and trotted toward Brandon who was sitting alone on the porch.

"I was wondering where you were," Brandon said cheerfully. "Figured you'd probably gone into town."

"You were right. Where are Robyn and Colby?"

"Dad hasn't come back yet. And Robyn took a book and went off into the woods to read again. Said she wanted to be alone for a while." Brandon looked at Diana. "She's not real happy with the idea of waiting a little while longer before we make up our minds about marriage, you know. And she's bored. Said she wants me to take her back to Portland."

"That might be a good idea under the circumstances," Diana said quietly.

Then it hit her that Robyn was gone again, vanished into the woods with a book. Robyn had never been around during the periods when an intruder had been rearranging things in Diana's cottage.

And the angry young woman could conceivably believe she had a motive to get even with Diana.

"Yeah, that's what I thought, too," Brandon was saying. "I told her I'd drive her back tomorrow." He got out of his chair. "You want some lunch?"

"Sounds good, but I think I'll wait," Diana said quickly. "I want to run back to my cottage for a few minutes. Uh, Brandon?"

"Yeah?" He was opening the screen door.

"Do you happen to know if Robyn is still reading *Shock Value*?" As soon as she had asked the question, Diana would have given a fortune to be able to call back the words. Brandon was as bright as his father at times.

Brandon slowly turned to look at her, wariness and concern in his dark eyes. "That's the book she took with her a little while ago."

Diana tried to pass it off lightly. "One of these days, I'm going to have to finish that book myself. Colby is getting impatient. I keep telling him that it's his fault it scares me to death, but I know he doesn't think that's much of an excuse. I'll be back in a few minutes, Brandon. If you're making tuna, make enough for me."

Brandon walked to the edge of the porch. "Why aren't you taking the car if you're in a hurry, Diana?"

"The walk will do me good." She started down the steps.

"Diana, wait! I'll come with you."

She whirled to face him. "I don't know if that's such a good idea, Brandon."

He gave her a keen glance. "I want to know, too. I have a right to know if Robyn's the one."

Diana stared at him helplessly. "Brandon, I'm just going to pick up a few items I left behind last night. There's no need for you to come along."

"You're going to see if someone's played another prank, aren't you? And you think that someone might be Robyn. She's out there in the woods alone with her copy of *Shock Value*. This is the second time she's read that book and she knows it very well. She also knows you're reading it."

Diana drew a deep breath. "Brandon, please, listen to me. I'm just going to pick up a few things I need. That's all."

"She could have done it," Brandon said slowly. "On the other two occasions the pranks were staged, she's been off by herself somewhere."

Diana gave up and started walking briskly along the road. Specter trotted close, sensing the change in the atmosphere. "I don't think she would do such things," Diana said after a moment. "I really don't."

"I'm not so sure," Brandon said with a calm that disturbed Diana. "She's got a motive. She really dislikes you. Blames you in some way for having made me think more carefully about getting married."

"Be careful, Brandon. Don't say things you'll regret later." Diana didn't like the new trace of cynicism she heard in his voice. It reminded her too much of his father. But maybe a certain degree of cynicism was inevitable in the growing-up process.

They walked in silence until the cottage came in sight. And then, when they were a few yards up the drive, Specter suddenly came to attention. The dog began barking loudly. He leaped up the steps and nosed the front door.

"There's someone inside," Diana said, feeling a cold sweat break out under her arms.

"Specter's tail is wagging," Brandon observed quickly.

Diana frowned. "That means he must know whoever it is who's in there."

"Maybe it's Dad." Brandon's relief was obvious as he dashed up the steps. "Maybe he stopped by to pick up your things for you."

"There's no sign of the Jeep," Diana said as she put the key into the lock.

The back door slammed just as Specter dashed into the hall. The dog raced into the kitchen, searching for his familiar quarry. Diana ran after him and promptly went sprawling as she tripped over a pile of garbage that had been left just inside the doorway.

"Are you all right?" Brandon demanded, pausing only for a second.

"Yes." Diana heaved herself up out of the mass of old coffee grounds, wet paper towels and vegetable peelings. "Let Specter out the back."

"Right." Brandon was already opening the back door. Specter hurried through, barking excitedly. Brandon followed the dog at a run, and Diana dashed after both of them.

She caught a brief glimpse of a running figure before it disappeared into the trees. The dog was hot on the intruder's heels. Brandon and Diana followed the sound of loud yipping and the equally loud sound of someone crashing through the undergrowth.

It was all over in a matter of minutes. The intruder didn't stand a chance of outrunning the dog and must have known it. Diana and Brandon raced into a small clearing a short time later and saw Specter panting heavily over Robyn Lambert's huddled, weeping figure.

"Robyn." Brandon looked stricken. Gone was his earlier dash of adult cynicism. He walked up to the girl slowly. "Why?"

Robyn lifted her tear-stained face from her arms and glared at Diana with anguish and rage. "It's her fault. You would have married me if it hadn't been for her."

"Oh, Robyn," Diana said softly.

"I know your Dad was against our getting married, Brandon. But we both knew that in the beginning. You were willing to stand up to him, you said. You wouldn't let him tell you what to do, you said. But then he stopped trying to order you around, and he started talking to you and you *listened* to him. She's the one who told him what to say to you. I know she is. She thinks she's so damn clever."

"Geez, Robyn." Brandon sounded thoroughly disgusted.

"And you listened to her, too, just like he did. You believed all that stuff she said about a woman having a career and being able to take care of herself. You quoted her to me, damn you. She put the words in your mouth. You said it would be best for me if we waited—but I know the truth. She talked you out of marrying me."

"That's enough, Robyn." Brandon reached down to help her to her feet.

Robyn lashed out at him with her hand. "Don't touch me, you bastard. I don't want you to ever touch me again. Who do you think you are, anyway? You're nobody, do you understand? Just the son of an ex-construction worker who writes cheap thrillers. My father is a lot richer than your father. He's got a college degree and he belongs to the right clubs, and he and Mom go to parties with the most important people in Portland. My parents were right. You aren't good enough for me."

Brandon's expression was frozen. "I had a close call, didn't I? The thought of being married to the kind of selfish, vicious little creep who would pull the kind of stunts you've been pulling on Diana is enough to make a man stay single for life." He turned and started walking back toward the cottage. "Come on. Let's get your things together. I'll drive you back to Portland this afternoon."

"*Brandon.* I love you."

"No you don't," Brandon said with astonishing wisdom. "You're just trying to find some guy who will marry you so you can get out of your parents' house. Any man will do. But if you had any brains, any self-respect, you'd move out by yourself. You'd learn to deal with things on your own. You just want someone to take care of you and make everything easy for you. Find another patsy."

"*Brandon.*" When Brandon didn't respond, Robyn swung around and confronted Diana. "It's all your fault. Brandon was going to marry me until you got involved. You ruined everything."

Diana stepped forward impulsively and put her arms around the young woman. Robyn pushed violently against her and then collapsed, weeping, on Diana's shoulder.

A long time later, when Robyn's tears had finally dried, Diana turned to find Colby standing quietly in the trees behind them. Without a word he led them both toward the cottage.

"CHAPTER TWELVE of *Shock Value*," Colby explained an hour later as he and Diana sat eating tuna sandwiches alone on the front porch. "Donnelly gets up in the middle of the night and falls into a pile of dirt taken from a freshly dug grave. Guess Robyn couldn't find any freshly dug graves and decided to make do with garbage."

"I hadn't gotten quite that far," Diana admitted. "I'm still on Chapter Ten. That poor girl. She's got some major problems."

"They're her problems, not ours and definitely not Brandon's. She was trying to use him."

"To escape her domineering family."

"Everybody's got something to escape," Colby said coolly. "It takes a while to learn that the only way you can really escape anything is to cut yourself free. You can't use other people to do the dirty work for you."

Diana concentrated on her sandwich. "No, I suppose not. Still, I feel sorry for her."

"After what she did to you? She deliberately tried to terrorize you, honey. In my book that means she's not entitled to any sympathy."

"You can be very hard at times, Colby."

He scowled at her and took a huge bite out of his sandwich. "Don't try to make me feel sorry for that little twit."

Diana decided to let the subject drop. She knew Colby's loyalties were limited but extremely fierce. His son was far more important to him than some neurotic little teenager who thought marriage was the ticket to freedom. Diana wondered exactly where she ranked on Colby's list of loyalties. She needed to know because something told her that very soon she was going to have to make a major decision.

"Is Brandon coming back tonight?"

"He said he was. Two hours to get to Portland, drop off Robyn and two hours to get back. He should be back here around seven."

"How did your visit with Gil Thorp go?"

"Maybe I'll have him and his wife out here for dinner one of these days. Is that okay with you?"

Diana smiled. "Certainly."

Colby was silent for a while, chewing reflectively. "He hadn't heard anything about the pranks."

"That stands to reason, since Robyn was behind them. She doesn't know anyone in town and therefore wouldn't have confided in anyone locally."

"Yeah."

Diana frowned slightly. "Colby, is something wrong?"

He shook his head. "Not any longer. The only thing that's bugging me is that Robyn is getting off damned light for what she did."

"She doesn't see it that way. She wanted marriage in the worst way, and now she's missed her chance with Brandon."

"Thank God."

BRANDON WALKED INTO THE HOUSE shortly after seven. Colby took one look at his son's haggard face and headed for the kitchen. He opened the refrigerator, took out a six-pack and returned to the living room.

"You want to go outside and sit on the porch for a while?" he asked his son.

Brandon looked up wearily. He nodded and got to his feet.

Diana settled back against the sofa and picked up *Shock Value*. "You two go on," she said easily. "I'm going to get through this book if it kills me."

Colby gave her a faint smile. The woman understood things, he thought. They didn't have to be spelled out for her. She knew that right now he needed to talk to Brandon alone.

It was crisp out on the porch but not too cold for a couple of macho males who happened to have a six-pack handy. Colby opened two cans and handed one to his son.

"There are times in a man's life," Colby said, "when the one thing he needs most in the world is a beer."

"Yeah."

"Rough drive back to Portland?"

"Yeah. I hurt her bad."

"And she hurt you just as bad."

"She wasn't the kind of girl I thought she was." Brandon looked perplexed. "I mean, she always seemed so sweet and helpless. I couldn't believe it when I realized it was her running out of Diana's house today. I wonder how Diana guessed about Robyn?"

"Diana's pretty sharp."

"Robyn blamed her for everything going wrong. But it was my fault, wasn't it?"

Colby shook his head. "You changed your mind about rushing into marriage. Everyone's got a right to do that. That's why it's a good idea to take your time about it. That's why you have to leave your options open until you're very sure of what you want."

Brandon grimaced. "Translated, that means you have to be careful about not getting the girl pregnant until you know damned well you want to marry her."

Colby shrugged. "Pregnancy has a way of closing down options, all right."

"Do you ever regret getting stuck with me?"

"Hell, no. Not for a minute. You're the best thing that ever happened to me, Brandon. If it hadn't been for you, I might have wound up in jail or in a gutter somewhere. You're the one who taught me the meaning of responsibility. You're the one who gave me something to work for. No, I don't regret having you. I just wish I'd been a little older and wiser when I did get you. As it was, you had to teach me about fatherhood, too."

"No," said Brandon after a long pull on his beer. "I didn't have to teach you about fatherhood. You're a natural. Too bad you didn't have some more kids somewhere along the line. You're wasting your talent in that department."

Colby felt an unexpected paternal warmth well up inside him. His voice became a little gruff. "Thanks, kid. I guess we both turned out okay, huh?"

"Yeah. I guess so."

"What you went through with Robyn was a very difficult situation. I want you to know I think you handled it damned well."

"I should never have gotten into it in the first place."

Colby grinned faintly. "Son, let me tell you something. Whenever you're talking about women, you're talking about difficult situations. They go together like fleas and dogs. You don't get one without the other."

Brandon smiled for the first time since he had walked in the door. "I'll remember that. By the way, just for the record, there was never any danger of me getting Robyn pregnant."

Colby nodded. "Glad to hear it."

"Not because I wasn't using precautions," Brandon said deliberately. "Although I would have if we'd ever done it. I'm not stupid. But we never did. Do it, that is. She said we had to wait until we were married. She kept telling me how good it was going to be after we were married. She really had me going."

Colby raised his brows inquiringly. "You're telling me I misinterpreted that little scene of you coming out of her bedroom the other morning?"

"I was in there, all right. But it was just the usual heavy make-out session. I was planning on going back to my own room before you, uh, got home, but I fell asleep."

"I apologize for jumping down your throat that morning." Colby shoved his fingers through his hair. "Seems like I've been doing a lot of apologizing lately. First to Diana and now you."

"There's something else I wanted to tell you, Dad."

"What's that?"

"Robyn swore over and over again during the drive back to Portland that the only prank she staged was the last one with the garbage. She claims she got the idea of doing something out of *Shock Value* after hearing about the other two incidents."

Colby gave Brandon a level look. "Do you believe her?"

Brandon looked thoughtful. "I know there's no reason to believe her, not after what she pulled. But for some reason, I think that this time she may have been telling the truth."

"Difficult situation," Colby mused.

"Do you think we should tell Diana?"

"No, she's got enough on her mind as it is."

"Like what?" Brandon asked curiously.

"I'm waiting for her to tell me."

SHE COULDN'T WAIT any longer. She was sure. It wasn't just that she was several days late—it was that she had a *feeling*. Somehow she knew for certain she was pregnant. The knowledge existed within her on some deep level that defied rational analysis. She stared down at the calendar in her hand, and the little numbers and days blurred together.

"You're not supposed to count the days when you're on a vacation, honey." Colby walked up behind her and put his arms around her. He deftly removed the calendar from her fingers. "Or is something more important going on here?"

"More important?" She was nervous, she realized. Far more nervous than she would be if she were interviewing for a new position.

"Am I about to overlook your birthday?" He smiled wickedly and nuzzled her neck. "Don't worry, I can come up with a terrific gift on very short notice."

"My birthday isn't until November."

"That's all right, my present can be unzipped early."

"You're supposed to be writing this morning."

He nibbled her ear. "I have already written great things this morning. I could use a break. Then I promise I will go back and write some more great things."

"Colby," Diana said very seriously. "Do you realize I don't even know when *your* birthday is?"

He stopped nibbling. "September second. Is that a problem?"

"No, of course not. It's just that it only goes to show there are a lot of things we still don't know about each other."

"We're both fast learners." He resumed munching her earlobe.

Diana took a deep breath. It was time to make her decision. "Colby, let's pack a lunch and go eat it on top of Chained Lady Falls."

"You talked me into it. A man can write great things any time. I'll make the sandwiches and pack the other essentials we always seem to need when we go to Chained Lady Falls." He gave her a quick, anticipatory leer and headed for the stairs that led to the bedroom.

Diana watched him go with a feeling of chagrin. She wondered if Colby even remembered the one time they had forgotten those essentials. He still hadn't mentioned what had happened that night they spent in the cave.

What if he denied his part in the whole thing? What if he honestly did not remember making love to her without taking precautions? What if he remembered but didn't want to believe she could have been so unlucky as to get pregnant the one and only time they had been careless?

What if he didn't want to share the responsibility with her?

The *what ifs* had been going through her mind for days now. They had intensified after Brandon had left to return to Portland. Diana had become increasingly tense as the reality of her pregnancy had begun to establish itself.

She knew Colby had noticed her preoccupation and the anxiety she had tried so hard to quell. Once or twice he had asked her if something was wrong but he'd stopped asking after she'd denied it.

"Don't forget we have Gil and his wife coming over for dinner tonight," Colby said as he came back downstairs. "We'll have to pick up some things in town after the picnic. I think you'll like Gil. He's a tough old character. Says what he thinks. Evelyn is his second wife. I don't know her very well, but she seems nice enough…" Colby broke off. "You okay, honey?"

Diana nodded quickly and turned toward the kitchen. "I'm fine. Let's get the sandwiches made."

Forty minutes later they reached the top of the falls. Diana immediately gave Specter a handful of his favorite dog biscuits, which he promptly wolfed down. Then he went off to check out the nearby woods while Colby spread the blanket on the ground.

"If you're going to make a habit of seducing me out here in the open, we may have to invest in an air mattress," he remarked as he finally settled the blanket on a patch of grass between two large boulders. "Either that, or you'll have to promise to always be on the bottom. At forty, a man starts to notice the rocks digging into his back."

"I'm crushed." Diana managed a smile as she unpacked the sandwiches. "Where's your sense of romance?"

"Where it always is. Right inside my jeans." He lowered himself into a sitting position beside her and reached for a sandwich. "I take it you want to eat first?"

Her fingers clenched around her sandwich. "To tell you the truth, I'd like to talk to you first."

"You're going to leave dents in that sandwich if you don't relax," Colby said with astonishing gentleness. He reached over and removed the sandwich from her hand. His gaze was intent and watchful. The teasing mood was gone. "So talk, lady. I'm listening."

She looked at him for a long moment and then she looked away, staring unseeingly at the landscape below. Unconsciously she wrapped her arms around her drawn-up knees.

"Colby, we've got a problem."

"We?"

She went cold and closed her eyes. "Maybe it would be more accurate under the circumstances to say I've got a problem. I'm pregnant."

"So that's it." He took a large bite out of his sandwich and chewed with enthusiasm. "I was wondering why you've been acting as if you were walking around in a mine field."

Diana heard the unconcerned tone in his voice and thought she would lose control and burst into tears right there in front of him. He didn't care because he didn't consider her pregnancy his problem.

She had made a huge mistake. She had been wrong, all wrong, to tell him. She should have kept it to herself. She should have handled her problems alone, just as she always did. In the end, a woman could only rely on herself. She'd always known that. Why had she allowed Colby Savagar to make her think there might be a few exceptions to that rule?

"It was that night in the cave, wasn't it?" Colby asked around a mouthful of sandwich.

"Yes. I thought you didn't remember. You never said anything." Diana didn't look at him. She could barely keep her voice steady. A sense of panic was setting in. She wanted to run, but she couldn't seem to move. Her stomach was in a knot. Her palms were damp. She certainly couldn't eat a single bite of her lunch now.

"I never said anything because you never mentioned it. I wasn't sure *you* remembered. I figured you'd bring it up if you wanted to discuss the situation. We were careless that night."

"Yes." At least he was noble enough to admit the fault had been mutual.

"You almost didn't tell me about the baby," Colby remarked musingly as he polished off the last of his sandwich. "You've been keeping all your fears and concerns to yourself, as usual. Tell me something, Diana. What made you decide to break the news today?"

"There was no point waiting any longer. I'm as sure as I can be without a test. I have to start making some decisions. Before I do that I need to know how you, uh, feel about the situation."

"Nice of you to include me in on the decision-making process, Madam Executive."

The edge that had appeared in his voice jolted her. Diana glanced at him nervously, unable to determine his mood. Colby's gaze was cool and direct. He was staring into her soul. "I'm sorry," she said a little helplessly.

"Yeah, so am I. Sorry it took you this long to tell me. Sorry you tried to shoulder the whole burden alone in your usual Diana-the-Amazon style. Sorry I didn't pin you down and wring the truth out of you earlier. I knew something was wrong. I shouldn't have let things go on this long. Ah, well. Live and learn. And I obviously still have a lot of things to learn about you, Diana."

Anger began to burn within her. Diana was grateful for it. It drove out some of the cold chill that had been creeping through her. "I'm sorry if I didn't handle this in exactly the way you think I should have handled it, but the fact is, I haven't had any experience along this line. I've been going crazy trying to figure out what to do."

His brows rose. "What's so damned hard about figuring out that the first thing you should have done was tell me?"

"Damn you, Colby." Diana brushed her wind-tousled hair back out of her eyes and looked at him with despair and rage. "I wasn't sure you'd want to know. We're involved in an affair that's only scheduled to last for the summer, remember?"

"Oh, Christ. Not that again. You're the one who always talks about our relationship as if it was scheduled only for the summer. I've told you a dozen times there's no need to put a time limit on it."

"Colby, this may come as a shock to you, but I have to make plans. I can't do that when everything's openended and casual. I need to know a few basic facts so I can organize my life. *I don't know the first thing about having a baby.*"

"Lucky for you, I do."

She stared at him. Some of the warmth began to return to her midsection. "What's that supposed to mean?"

"Just what it sounds like." He fished around inside the picnic basket for another sandwich. "I'm an expert on kids, remember? You want cheese or egg salad?"

"Neither. Colby, stop fooling around with the sandwiches and tell me exactly what you mean."

He looked at her. "Just what I said. Trust me, I know what I'm doing."

"I wish I did."

"Relax, honey. We'll take this one step at a time."

Diana searched his face. "What's the first step?"

"Simple. We get married."

Diana couldn't move for an instant. "I knew," she finally whispered. "Deep down inside, I knew you were different. I knew you would never run from something like this. Thank you, Colby. Your offer means more to me than I can possibly say." She dashed the back of her hand across her eyes to wipe away the moisture. Then she sniffed. "But I can't marry you."

"The hell you can't."

She threw herself into his arms, her eyes damp with more unshed tears. "Don't you understand? It wouldn't be right. Listen to me, Colby, I've thought about this a lot."

"Knowing you, honey, you've thought about it too much. You have a tendency to overanalyze things." His arms tightened roughly around her. "This is not a complicated situation, Diana. Don't try to make it complicated."

Her fingers clenched into the fabric of his shirt as she buried her face against his chest. "I can't put you through the same situation you were forced into twenty years ago. You've made it clear that once was enough.

I won't let history repeat itself for you. It's not fair. *It's just not fair.*"

"My sweet stubborn little amazon," Colby said into her hair. "History has nothing to do with this. And neither does fairness. We're talking about you and me. We're going to have a baby. That means we get married."

AT SUNSET the last of the sun's rays turned the waterfall first to gold and then to scarlet. Colby privately decided he'd never seen the veil of Chained Lady Falls look more like blood than it did that evening. A curious sense of rightness flowed through him.

For the first time since he had returned to Fulbrook Corners, he had the feeling that he was finally going to complete the unfinished business he sensed had brought him here.

Being an expectant father was playing tricks on his mind, he thought, amused. He had the oddest feeling that he was somehow holding both past and future in his hands, and that the link between the two was Diana.

Harlequin Temptation

COMING NEXT MONTH

CALLOWAY CORNERS

Created by four outstanding Superromance authors, bonded by lifelong friendship and a love of their home state: Sandra Canfield, Tracy Hughes, Katherine Burton and Penny Richards.

CALLOWAY CORNERS

Home of four sisters as different as the seasons, as elusive as the elements; an undiscovered part of Louisiana where time stands still and passion lasts forever.

CALLOWAY CORNERS

Birthplace of the unforgettable Calloway women: *Mariah*, free as the wind, and untamed until she meets the preacher who claims her, body and soul; *Jo*, the fiery, feisty defender of lost causes who loses her heart to a rock and roll man; *Tess*, gentle as a placid lake but tormented by her longing for the town's bad boy and *Eden*, the earth mother who's been so busy giving love she doesn't know how much she needs it until she's awakened by a drifter's kiss...

CALLOWAY CORNERS

Coming from Superromance, in 1989:
Mariah, by Sandra Canfield, a January release
Jo, by Tracy Hughes, a February release
Tess, by Katherine Burton, a March release
Eden, by Penny Richards, an April release

CALL-1

Have You Ever Wondered If You Could Write A Harlequin Novel?

Here's great news—Harlequin is offering a series of cassette tapes to help you do just that. Written by Harlequin editors, these tapes give practical advice on how to make your characters—and your story—come alive. There's a tape for each contemporary romance series Harlequin publishes.

Mail order only

All sales final

TEARS IN THE RAIN

STARRING
CHRISTOPHER CAVZENOVE AND
SHARON STONE

BASED ON A NOVEL BY
PAMELA WALLACE

PREMIERING IN NOVEMBER